LONG WAY DOWN

Frank's heart trip-hammered as the shot pierced the air. Up ahead, he saw Nancy dangling wildly on the end of her rope, high above the ravine.

"Nancy!" he shouted, his pace quickening to a mad dash that brought him to the mouth of the ravine. "Throw your weight! Swing toward me!"

For a long moment Nancy didn't seem to hear him. Then, gradually, she started to swing, trying to arc far enough to land beside Frank on the opposite side of the ravine.

"Hurry, Nancy," Frank said, glancing around for any sign of the gunman. Nancy swung farther with each effort. "Okay, when I say three, jump," Frank yelled excitedly. "One! Two!" The rope swung toward Frank, then away again.

"Three!" Frank held out his arms to catch her. He watched Nancy's hands let go of the rope. She fell in a smooth arc—down, down, down . . .

"Nancy! Watch out!"

Nancy Drew & Hardy Boys SuperMysteries

Available from ARCHWAY Paperbacks

A NANCY DREW and HARDY BOYS SUPER·MYSTERY™

SPIES AND LIES

Carolyn Keene

AN ARCHWAY PAPERBACK
Published by POCKET BOOKS
New York London Toronto Sydney Tokyo Singapore

This book is a work of fiction. Names, characters, places, and incidents are either products of the author's imagination or are used fictitiously. Any resemblance to actual events or locales or persons, living or dead, is entirely coincidental.

AN ARCHWAY PAPERBACK *Original*

 An Archway Paperback published by
POCKET BOOKS, a division of Simon & Schuster Inc.
1230 Avenue of the Americas, New York, NY 10020

Copyright © 1992 by Simon & Schuster Inc.
Produced by Mega-Books of New York, Inc.

ISBN: 0-671-73125-4

First Archway Paperback printing July 1992

10 9 8 7 6 5 4 3 2 1

Cover art by Frank Morris

Printed in the U.S.A.

IL 6+

Chapter

One

YOU CAN DO IT, Nancy!" Judy Noll called. "Just a few feet more!"

Nancy Drew gripped the thick rope in her hands and hauled her body several more painful inches up its length. Her muscles strained to hold her in place. She could feel sweat trickling down her sides under her sweat suit.

"It's not as easy as it—looks!" Nancy gasped. Already she had climbed nearly thirty feet above the floor of the FBI Training Academy's cavernous gym. She peered down at Judy standing far below and felt dizzy.

In a gray sweat suit like Nancy's and with her blond hair pulled up in a ponytail, Judy looked like a two-inch version of Nancy as she steadied the rope at the bottom. Several other women in regulation sweat suits performed calisthenics nearby. A group of young men jogged around the edge of the gym, sending echoes from the slap of shoes against wood resounding across the room.

"First time's the hardest," Nancy heard Judy call. She glanced down again and saw the athletic young woman give her a thumbs-up sign. "Go for it!"

Nancy focused her attention on the rope once again. She wished she had worked harder at her weekly aerobics sessions back home in River Heights. Nancy and her friend George Fayne had recently joined a class together. All the regular exercise in the world, Nancy suspected, still couldn't have prepared her for her training with the FBI.

Just a little farther, she reminded herself. *So far you're doing great.*

With a final surge of energy, Nancy yanked her body up the last two feet of the rope. She slapped the ring that held it at the top, making the metal clang against her palm.

"Way to go, Nancy!" The gym echoed with the sound of Judy's clapping. Nancy started to wave to her audience—and then froze. Judy had stepped back from the rope to applaud. That meant, Nancy realized, that the rope was—

"Whoa—!" Several dozen of Nancy's fellow trainees watched as her rope swung jerkily, sending Nancy half sliding, half falling all the way down to the floor of the gym in a few seconds.

She landed with a loud thump. "Are you okay?" she heard Judy cry. "I'm sorry—I just let go for a second. I didn't realize—"

"Don't worry about it." Nancy blew a loose strand of reddish blond hair out of her face and struggled to stand on shaky legs, rubbing her backside with a rueful grin. She heard new applause—loud and slow—and glanced over at the group of male joggers who had stopped running to witness her fall. The guys were grinning broadly. A tall, sandy-haired, good-looking man in the front gave Nancy a mock salute.

He must think I'm the world's biggest klutz, Nancy thought, feeling her face grow warm. She wondered who the recruit was. As an agent-in-training, he had to be at least five years older than Nancy—but he was awfully cute.

"I just burned my hands on the rope a little, that's all," she told Judy, turning away. "They told us when we applied for training that life with the FBI could be dangerous. It looks like they were right!"

"You were doing great until I goofed," Judy insisted loyally. "Especially considering the fact that you just got off a plane last night. The rest of us have been here two weeks already."

Nancy smiled. She had only met Judy that morning before breakfast, but she knew that the young woman took her training very seriously. Judy had a law degree, but she didn't consider that nearly as important as becoming a special agent for the FBI. Nancy couldn't help admiring her determination and drive. She also wondered why she of all people had been chosen to be Judy's bodyguard.

Then, though, this case had been weird from the very beginning, Nancy knew. It began with an urgent phone call from Special Agent Daniel Burr at dinner on Monday night. Agent Burr had told Nancy how much he admired her detective work, and asked whether she might help the bureau with an important case at their training academy.

It seemed that Judy Noll, one of the FBI's newest recruits, had been shot at a few nights earlier. Judy was the daughter of a very powerful senator—Sam Noll, of Iowa—Burr had explained. The previous Friday night Judy had been in her dorm room with a bad cold while the other trainees were attending a lecture. Two shots were fired through her bedroom window. Luckily, they missed Judy and landed in the wall behind her bed.

"But why call m-me?" Nancy had stammered, secretly thrilled at the idea of working for the bureau. She noticed that her father, Carson Drew, was listening carefully to her side of the conversation. "How can I help?"

"You're young and female," Burr had replied. "If you posed as a new trainee, we could pair you up with Judy without arousing suspicion. You'd act as her bodyguard while we investigated the case. And while you were at it, you could keep your ears open and find out whether any of the other recruits have a grudge against Judy. Because this case is so important, I've been given permission to handle it my way," Burr had added. "I've looked forward to working with you for a long time."

On Tuesday night Nancy was on a flight from Chicago to Washington, D.C. Agent Burr had picked her up at Dulles Airport, driven her the two hours to the academy, in Virginia, then outlined her mission in his office once they arrived. He had given Nancy the name Nancy Douglas and explained that she was to pose as a translator with a master's degree in French who had volunteered to help with a secret, very urgent FBI mission. Like all other agents, she would have to go through basic training. The urgency of her mission would explain why she had entered the training program two weeks late.

It was after midnight by the time Agent Burr had finished briefing her. Nancy had had time for only a few hours' sleep in the dorm before she was wakened at six to begin her daily routine—breakfast followed by two hours of physical training.

"I can't wait for afternoon classes," Nancy confided to Judy. "Gathering evidence, fingerprinting, cross-examining suspects—that's my kind of education!"

"What good does it do to know how to cross-examine someone if you're not physically fit enough to catch them?" Judy pointed out with a grin. "But don't worry, you may be a weakling today, but in a week you'll outclimb me."

"Speaking of which," Nancy teased, swinging her the rope, "it's your turn, pro."

Judy gave her a cocky grin. "Fine. I bet I can make it to the top in less than three min—" She was interrupted by a loud, shrill whistle.

"Noll! Douglas!" a voice roared.

Nancy turned to see Samantha Havlicek, their phys ed instructor, striding toward them.

"You two seem to be exercising your mouths more than your bodies," the woman commented in a sharp voice that Nancy thought perfectly matched her spotless sweat suit, gleaming white athletic shoes, and dark, no-nonsense braid.

"Agent Noll was just giving me some pointers," Nancy said. Burr had told her that trainees were called agents even though they hadn't graduated.

"I saw those 'pointers,'" Havlicek snapped. "Sliding down the rope like a monkey! What do you think this is, a playground? I don't know who pulled the strings to get you into the course this late, Douglas," she said to Nancy, "but don't think for a minute you'll get any special treatment from me. Fifty push-ups for both of you for disrupting training. Then Agent Noll will take a turn at the rope."

"She sure is tough," Judy grumbled after Havlicek had stalked off toward another pair of trainees.

"You can say that again." Nancy got down on the floor beside Judy to begin her push-ups. She glanced around to make sure none of the other trainees were close enough to hear her. "She sounded suspicious about my being here, don't you think? That last remark of hers was pretty unnerving."

"Don't worry. She's just mad." Judy started doing push-ups, and Nancy followed her lead. "At least she made us do this instead of running laps."

"What's wrong with laps?" Nancy blushed. "Haven't you noticed that cute guy over there?"

"Who, Jeff Abelson?" Judy sniffed. "I should warn you, Nancy, he's the world's biggest flirt. He's asked out practically every female here in the past two weeks, and the worst part is, each girl said yes. The only women he doesn't like are the ones who turn him down. I guess that's why he's been rude to me the past few days."

"You wouldn't go out with him?" Nancy gasped for air as she pushed herself up for the tenth time. "Why not?"

"I think he's just interested in me because of my father," Judy replied breezily. "I have to watch out for people like him—people who try to get close to me so they can ask a senator for a favor. He probably thinks that I can help him get a job in Washington. You know, Nancy, it's not easy being the daughter of a rich and powerful man. You always wonder who your real friends are."

"I hadn't really thought about that," Nancy said, suddenly uncomfortable.

"Of course not," Judy said. "Why should you? But, anyway, watch out for Jeff. I can tell he has his eye on you."

Embarrassed, Nancy concentrated on her exercises. She noticed that twenty-three-year-old Judy was having little trouble with her push-ups. Already, Judy had proved better at sit-ups, vaulting, and jumping jacks than Nancy. She reminded Nancy more of an Olympic athlete than a damsel in distress.

The night before Agent Burr had told Nancy why he had had to hire someone from outside the bureau to work on this case. The FBI had determined that the shots were fired from behind a tree outside Judy's window, though the shooter's footprints had been erased. Later analysis had determined that the bullets imbedded in the bedroom wall were academy issue. With no record of any outside visitors the night of the shooting, it appeared that the bullets must have been stolen from a locked cabinet at the firing range. That meant that the shooter was probably a trainee, an instructor, or possibly an agent who knew his or her way around the academy.

"Judy's not the most popular trainee we've ever had, but she's not hated," Burr had told Nancy. "The attack may have been aimed at hurting her father, but he claims he has no enemies who would do such a thing. In any case, until I know who shot those bullets, I can't afford to trust anyone here."

"Twenty-four, twenty-five—halfway there!" Judy gasped, momentarily interrupting Nancy's thoughts.

Nancy grimaced and kept pushing. She remembered Burr's look of relief when she'd said, "How do you want me to proceed?"

"We can't put you in the same dorm room as Judy because that would cause suspicion," he had answered. "But we can give the two of you the same training schedule. While we continue with our investigation, you stick close to Judy at all times, without drawing attention to the fact."

I wish he'd told me to bring along some vitamins, Nancy thought as she fought to match Judy's pace. She glanced at her partner and felt better. Drops of sweat had popped out on Judy's face and were dripping off the tip of her nose.

"Forty-nine, fifty!" Judy gasped.

"Alors!" Nancy cried, collapsing onto her stomach and hoping her high school French sounded okay. She was glad there wouldn't be any foreign language classes here, or she'd risk blowing her cover. Excited as she was about taking classes on criminal investigation, it was scary to think that one of her classmates might be the person who tried to hurt Judy.

"Not a bad show, kid." Nancy felt someone press a shoe into her lower back. Nancy pushed up, but the shoe refused to move. She arched her back finally and spun around, sending the owner of the shoe shooting backward. Standing up, Nancy saw that the woman was her roommate, Marianne Risi.

"Oh! Sorry," Nancy said as Marianne continued to stumble backward. Marianne was a few inches shorter than Nancy, but she was fit and strong. Her brown, curly hair was held in place with a blue headband. Her dark eyes seemed anything but friendly now that she had landed on the floor.

Nancy extended her hand to help Marianne up. "You must be Agent Risi. I'm your roommate, Nancy Douglas. I'm sorry we didn't get a chance to meet before. You were asleep when I got in last night, and you left this morning before I woke up."

"I make a habit of working out early." Marianne refused Nancy's help as she stood upright. "You won't get anywhere in the bureau if you sleep in till six o'clock."

Nancy blushed. "It's m-my first day here," she stammered. "I guess I didn't realize we were supposed to—"

"Come on, Nancy," Judy interrupted, getting up from the mat. "It's my turn to climb that rope."

Marianne turned to smirk at Judy. "What's the matter, Noll? You don't like your servant taking time off to talk to someone else?"

"Lay off it, Marianne," Judy said smoothly. "We're supposed to be working out, that's all."

"Why bother? When push comes to shove, Daddy can probably work you into any job you want in the FBI anyway. You might as well cut class and go have a milk shake with your little friend here."

"See you later, Marianne."

Judy stalked away with Nancy following. "What was that all about?" Nancy asked.

"She's just a creep," Judy told her partner. "Too bad they put you in with her. Her last roommate quit the academy after just three days. She said it was too much pressure. I bet I know where some of that pressure came from."

"She seems to resent you especially," Nancy pointed out.

"She's like that with everyone, I think," Judy said. "She finds your weak spot and homes in on it. Of course, she tries hardest to get to me, since I'm her main competition for top rating in the class."

Nancy shook her head. The gym was full of competitive trainees all determined to let nothing—and no one—get in their way. Nancy guessed some of them might be pretty outraged if they thought Judy had an advantage over them because of her father's influence. As far as Nancy could tell, though, Judy played fair.

"Let's use that rope in the corner." Judy pointed to a part of the gym that was almost empty. "We'll be able to talk there."

Nancy followed Judy to the rope and steadied it for her.

11

"Wish me luck," Judy said with a smile.

"You bet!" Nancy replied. She watched Judy begin her climb. After all those push-ups, Nancy knew that even Judy's arms had to be aching, but the trainee didn't hesitate for a second. Nancy admired the ease with which Judy pulled herself steadily up to the ceiling. Clearly Judy was determined that not even a gunman was going to get in her way.

"You're almost there, Judy!" Nancy called as the young woman inched closer to the top.

"Nancy, something's not . . ." Judy began, her voice trailing off before she screamed.

Nancy looked up. Judy was grasping frantically at the rope with one hand. To her horror, Nancy saw that a section of rope right above Judy's head was frayed. Judy was barely hanging on by a thread!

"Hold on, Judy!" Nancy called. It was too late. Nancy felt the rope grow slack and loosen in her grasp. Judy let out a scream and plummeted!

Chapter

Two

NANCY BARELY HAD TIME to think. She ran under Judy to try to cushion the girl's fall. The full weight of the older girl fell on Nancy, sending them both crashing to the floor.

"Are you all right?" Nancy asked, pushing herself up off the ground.

"I think so," Judy responded between gulps of air. "I'm just shaken up, that's all, but you could have been killed by me."

As Nancy helped Judy to her feet, a whistle of appreciation sounded behind them. Nancy wasn't surprised to see Marianne standing there, a smirk on her face. "Bravo, Judy! I bet the bureau can't wait to put you to work. What did you say your specialty was? Slapstick comedy?"

Nancy couldn't believe how cold Marianne was being. "Slapstick had nothing to do with this!" Nancy said, picking the rope up from the ground. "Judy's lucky she wasn't killed."

"I'm not surprised she brought the rope down," Marianne said as a crowd of trainees, both male and female, rushed to the scene of the accident. "Noll could stand to lose a few pounds."

"Watch yourself, Risi—" Judy protested, red-faced. Nancy could tell by the tense set of Judy's jaw that she was ready to snap. Still, Nancy knew that Judy probably wouldn't say or do anything to jeopardize her place at the academy.

The sharp blare of Samantha Havlicek's whistle broke through the tension. For the first time all morning, Nancy was glad to hear it.

"Any injuries, Noll?" the instructor asked, moving quickly to Judy's side and examining her.

"I'm fine, thanks to Agent Douglas. She broke my fall." Judy smiled grimly at Nancy.

Havlicek nodded, then turned to the crowd behind them. "Okay, spectators, hit the mats. You NATS can do thirty push-ups."

Gnats? Nancy wondered briefly. Then she remembered that NATS stood for New Agents in Training—the formal title for trainees. As the group hustled to the mats, Nancy examined the frayed end of the rope. Havlicek approached her.

"This should be good practice for you,

Douglas," the instructor said. "What do you think made the rope snap like that?"

"I hate to guess," Nancy replied. "At first glance, you might think the fibers had worn through, but the rope is too new. And see the ends where the break is? They're smooth, and all about the same length."

"Are you saying what I think you're saying?" Judy interjected, turning pale.

"I think the rope may have been cut." Nancy looked at Havlicek, who raised an eyebrow skeptically.

"Cut! Not again—!" Judy began.

"This could be related to the attack on Friday —the one you told me about this morning," Nancy said, not wanting to break her cover in front of Havlicek. "On the other hand, it doesn't make sense. That attack on Friday was aimed specifically at you. But anybody in the gym could have climbed this rope."

"I agree, but I think the incident should be reported," Havlicek said. "Noll, who's the agent in charge of your case?"

"Agent Burr," Judy replied.

"I'll notify him and make sure this rope is sent to forensics," Havlicek said. The instructor sighed. "Agent Noll, I understand your decision to remain in the academy. But I have to confess that your stubbornness concerns me, especially when it affects my course. I wish you'd take some friendly advice and reconsider."

"Thanks for your advice, Agent Havlicek," Judy said coolly. "But no matter how hard it gets, I'm determined to complete the term."

"I expected as much," Havlicek replied. Then she blew a short note on her whistle. "Okay, time to hit the showers."

As she and Judy joined the other recruits, Judy slowed down and whispered, "Uh-oh, more trouble ahead." Nancy turned to see one of the male trainees headed their way. Instantly she felt her face grow warm.

"I told you he had his eye on you," Judy murmured.

"You said he moved fast," Nancy admitted. "But I didn't know you meant *this* fast."

"Judy, that was some dive you took off that rope," Jeff Abelson said as he approached the two girls. Nancy noted that he was even more handsome up close. About twenty-five years old, he had clear, sea green eyes, and his smile revealed a dimple in one cheek. "You're okay, though, right?" he added.

"Why the sudden concern, Jeff?" Judy remarked. "Were you wondering who the new kid in town is, perhaps?"

"Well, yes, actually." Jeff flashed an uncertain smile at Judy. "I *was* hoping you'd introduce me to your savior here."

Judy rolled her eyes. "Agent Jeff Abelson, meet Agent Nancy Douglas."

"Hello," Nancy said, taking Jeff's outstretched hand. Abelson smiled into her eyes, and Nancy understood why so many trainees had agreed to go out with him.

"You were a real hero out there, Douglas. Judy's lucky you were around," Jeff said. He turned back to Judy, and his expression turned serious. "You know, it looks like somebody's out to get you, Judy."

"I guess it does," Judy said, rolling her eyes.

Nancy saw confusion flash across Jeff's face. He didn't seem to understand why Judy was angry. "Do you have any idea who might do a thing like this?" she asked the young man.

"Not offhand, but if you want, I could think about it for a while, and we could meet for dinner to talk it over."

"Um, I think we'd better hit those showers now, Nancy," Judy said, grabbing Nancy's arm and hustling her off.

Jeff laughed and backed away. "I get the hint. See you around campus, Agent Douglas." He turned and headed toward the men's locker room.

"What did you do that for?" Nancy asked her partner as they entered the steamy women's dressing room and opened their lockers. "He might have come up with a valuable clue."

"Believe me, Nancy, he just wants to make another conquest," Judy answered.

Nancy frowned. Judy sounds jealous, she realized. Jeff doesn't seem anything like she described him.

17

"Well, he certainly is cute," Nancy pointed out.

"I suppose," Judy snapped. "But until the bureau catches my attacker, I'm not trusting anyone—no matter what he looks like."

Without another word, she disappeared into a shower stall.

Nancy felt guilty for forgetting Judy's situation —even if for only an instant. Gathering up her towel, she entered the stall next to Judy's. The water felt cool and refreshing.

Abelson—Jeff Abelson, Nancy thought. The name sounded familiar. Her eyes flew open as she remembered. Burr had brought up his name the night before. She remembered Burr telling her that several witnesses had seen a trainee leave the Friday night lecture early—a young agent named Jeff Abelson.

Maybe Judy's right about him, Nancy thought reluctantly as she toweled off and began to dress. She decided that during her free time she'd take a closer look at the file Burr had given her. Until then, though, she would be busy with another lecture, a quick lunch, and the four hours of firearms training that were required of the trainees every day.

In the mirror Nancy inspected the tan slacks, white blouse, and tan cotton blazer she'd chosen to wear on her first day of school. NATS were required to wear business attire to class. Nancy hoped her clothes made her look as sophisticated as the college graduates with whom she was training. She removed her jacket and strapped the holster Burr had given her on her belt. Then she reluctantly picked up the .38-caliber pistol she had kept in her locker during PE.

Burr had told her that the gun was called a red handle, and that all trainees were required to carry them. The guns' handles were painted red, indicating that they couldn't be shot because their firing pins had been removed. The trainees were supposed to get used to the feel of carrying a weapon at all times.

Nancy shuddered, glancing at the gun. She knew she would never get used to it—certainly not in the short time she would be at the academy. She had always hated guns and their potential for violence. But she was posing as a trainee, and she would be tested on firearms use as all the other trainees were. Later, on the firing range, she knew she would be using a loaded gun.

"Come on, Nancy. If we're late for the lecture, we'll really catch it," Judy said, interrupting her thoughts.

"I'm ready," Nancy said. The two left the gym and began the trek across the campus to the forensics lab. In the bright daylight Nancy thought the campus was very impressive. Large, modern concrete buildings formed a neat square with a green lawn in the center. Shade trees lined the paths between the buildings. Nancy had just about memorized the map Burr had given her.

"Whew, it's hot out here! Give me a second, Nancy," Judy said, running toward a water fountain just outside the lab.

"Sure, Judy," Nancy said. She waited on the front steps, checking out the trainees walking by.

It was strange to think that someone on this superefficient campus was actually stalking a young, ambitious woman like Judy Noll. Nancy peered around at the shady corners and brightly lit lawn, wondering where the attacker was at this moment. Suddenly she felt an iron grip on her shoulder.

"Hey!" Nancy shrieked, trying to turn to face her attacker.

The steely grip prevented her from moving. Nancy's eyes widened as she felt her assailant's warm breath against her ear.

"Don't look now," a harsh voice whispered. "I know who you really are!"

Chapter

Three

FRANK HARDY couldn't help smiling as his old friend spun around. He had to admit he had been surprised when he spotted Nancy in the gym, but not shocked. Frank and his younger brother, Joe, had been involved in many cases, and this wasn't the first time they had run into Nancy during one of their investigations.

"Fancy meeting you here, Nancy," he said.

"Frank!" Nancy said, relief sweeping across her face. Then she saw Joe Hardy right behind his brother. "I don't know whether to slug you or hug you."

"I'll take the hug, please," Joe said.

Frank noticed Judy Noll walking toward them

with a puzzled expression on her face. "Hi," he said loudly, letting the other two know that Judy was there. "You're Agent Noll, right? I've seen you around campus."

"I've noticed you guys, too." Judy shook hands with Frank and Joe, eyeing them curiously. "You know Nancy?"

"We were counselors at the same summer camp a couple of years ago," Joe chimed in creatively. "My name is Hill. Joe Hill. This is my brother, Frank."

Frank glanced toward Nancy, who winked to show she had registered the Hardys' alias. "I never would have believed the Hill brothers would end up working for the FBI," she couldn't resist teasing. "Judy, you wouldn't believe how those eight-year-old campers had Frank and Joe wrapped around their little fingers."

"Sounds like fun." Judy was smiling at Joe with interest. Frank wasn't surprised to see Joe smiling back. With her thick blond hair and slim, athletic build, Judy was very attractive.

"We're on our way to forensics class," Nancy said. "Will you join us?"

"We're going to stay out in the sun a few more minutes," Frank said. "The air-conditioning is murderous."

"Good idea," Nancy said quickly. "We'll see you in a few minutes then."

Frank watched the girls walk toward the lab and saw Nancy gesture behind Judy's back for the brothers to stay where they were. "She'll be back in a minute," he told his brother. He glanced at a small knot of students talking nearby. "Let's wait over there by those trees. We won't want to be overheard when she comes back."

"So what's the story?" Joe asked as they sat down under an oak tree. Joe loosened his tie and took off his jacket to cool off. "Don't tell me Nancy's joined the FBI!"

"Impossible," Frank said with a laugh. "She's not old enough. She must be undercover, like you and me."

"You don't think she's working on the same case, do you?"

"I guess we'll find out soon." Frank pointed to Nancy, who was making her way back to them.

"Thanks for not blowing my cover, guys," Nancy murmured breathlessly as she joined the Hardys, "but Judy knows about me. For your information, in front of anyone else, my last name is Douglas. I'm a translator on a special mission. And I have a master's degree in French."

"Ooh-la-la!" trilled Joe. "That was fast. Weren't you in high school just last year?"

"It's great to see you again, Nancy," Frank said, interrupting his brother. "We don't have much time before class starts. Can you tell us what you're doing here—or is that top secret?"

Nancy briefly explained that she had been brought in as Judy's bodyguard.

Joe let out a low whistle. "Pretty impressive. I

should have figured you were working on that case when I saw you with Judy."

"We've actually been wondering if the attack on Judy has something to do with our case," Frank added, running a hand through his dark hair.

"What *is* your case, or is it top secret?" Nancy asked.

"The Network sent us," Frank said. He had discussed the top secret U.S. organization with Nancy before. Network agents had successfully defeated terrorist groups, smugglers, and other criminal coalitions in the past. The Hardys' Network contact was an agent called the Gray Man. "You know we've worked for them from time to time."

Nancy nodded.

"Did Burr say anything about Autowatch?" Frank asked. "Or was it mentioned in any of your background information?"

Nancy thought for a minute. "It sounds familiar. It's some kind of FBI watchdog operation, right?"

"Exactly," Frank said. "Ten years ago several major U.S. auto companies were suspected of unfair trade practices. They were buying huge amounts of steel and other materials from foreign countries—more than is allowed under America's trade agreements. The FBI set up Autowatch to keep an eye on the industry and keep the companies in line."

"Was it successful?" Nancy asked.

"Yes, until recently," Frank told her. "The Network discovered a cover-up. Some of the companies were continuing to break the trade laws—and a few employees of Autowatch were looking the other way, even concealing information. The agents involved were recent graduates of this academy."

"That's where we come in," said Joe. "We're supposed to be computer specialists. We're the bait."

"I see. The Network is hoping that the guys running the cover-up will try to recruit you for Autowatch and get you to work for them," Nancy said.

"Right," Frank said. "The Network figures that likely recruits are ones vulnerable to large cash offers or in danger of failing the training. Either might cooperate to get ahead."

"I have the easy job," Joe said, grinning. "I get to fail a bunch of tests. No sweat."

"And I'm the money-hungry one," Frank said. "But that's not our only job. The Network strongly suspects that the person doing the recruiting works at the academy, most likely as an instructor. We're supposed to check out all the instructors, plus keep an eye out for any likely trainees who might be targeted."

"That's why we thought Judy might have something to do with all this," Joe put in. "We thought she had been recruited, and then threatened to tell the authorities. Did Burr mention anything about the recruiting scam to you?"

"Nothing," Nancy said. "But I'll be sure to let you know if he does."

"Great," Frank said. He glanced back at the group on the stairs. A couple of the trainees were staring curiously at him. "But don't let him know our real identities," Frank said to Nancy, lowering his voice. "No one in the FBI knows who we are. The Network did an amazing job with faking our backgrounds. We had to go through some pretty intense screening to get accepted here."

"You can count on me," Nancy said. She glanced at her watch. "We'd better get to class."

Frank followed Nancy and Joe into the forensics lab. For one hour each day he and Joe had attended forensics class with the other trainees. The week before, the lectures had focused on the history of the bureau and the FBI's jurisdiction. This week they were learning fingerprinting techniques.

"I'm glad I get to be the failure. This technical jargon gives me a headache," Joe said as he took a seat at one of the long, white tables in the lab.

Frank took the seat next to him and watched Nancy sit down next to Judy two rows up. "You should try paying attention—this stuff can be really fascinating."

"There are plenty of other things to pay attention to." Joe flashed a smile at a petite brunette woman sitting at the table in front of them. "Hi, Audrey," he said, touching her shoulder.

She turned around. "Hi, Joe. Hi, Frank." She smiled at them.

"First Judy, now Audrey. Can't you keep your mind on a case without coming on to every girl you meet?" Frank asked in a whisper.

"Sure," Joe whispered back. "But why?"

The class quieted down as the instructor, Arnold Hoffman, entered the room. His graying hair, neat salt-and-pepper beard, and wire-rimmed bifocals made him look smart and distinguished. Hoffman's Network file showed that he had been with the bureau for fifteen years.

"Good morning, agents," Hoffman addressed the class. "Today we learn about latent fingerprints."

Frank listened with interest as the instructor explained that latent prints were prints you couldn't see—they could be left on almost any surface. "Until recently, latent prints were difficult to retrieve from absorbent surfaces such as paper," Hoffman explained. "But with laser technology, we can photograph the hidden print without damaging it."

The instructor walked to a large machine in the corner—a laser fingerprint reader. It looked almost like a photocopy machine, Frank thought, except that a camera-like apparatus hovered over the center. Frank was thrilled to be learning the latest detection techniques from the top experts in the country.

As Hoffman continued to lecture, Joe scanned the students' faces. He had tried to get to know a little about each of them since he and Frank had arrived. Most of the trainees were in their mid-twenties. They were all smart and determined. Frank had found few who fit the Network profile. Nevertheless, there had to be at least one candidate, he thought bitterly.

"Hey, Frank, lecture's over," Joe said, nudging his brother. "It's my favorite time of day. Lunchtime."

"Not yet, Joe," Frank said. He lowered his voice. "First we have to lay out some bait, remember?"

Forcing himself to look disgusted, Frank gathered up his books and sauntered out of the building. Joe stomped after him to the front steps.

"You really bug me, you know?" Joe shouted, jabbing a finger into Frank's chest. "You've got a lousy attitude."

"Shut up, Joe," Frank snapped. "I told you I don't see the point of this class."

Frank was pleased to see that the argument had already attracted the attention of at least two NATS. One was Audrey LaFehr, the agent Joe had spoken to in the lab. The other was Erin Seward, a pretty, green-eyed blond woman who Frank knew was Judy Noll's roommate. The two women seemed to be exact opposites, Frank noted. Erin was as cool and distant as Audrey was warm and friendly.

"Learning something new won't kill you. Money isn't all there is, you know," Joe said, pretending to try to lower his voice.

"Maybe not," Frank retorted, "but it's sure hard to live without it."

"Hey, what's with you two?" Audrey asked, laying a hand on Frank's arm.

Joe scowled. "Frank's having second thoughts about the academy," he said.

"It's just that someone with my computer smarts could make lots more money doing something else," Frank snapped.

"All you ever think about is money!" Joe shouted.

"Try living without it," Frank said stuffily. "I signed up because I figured I'd be appreciated for my talents and offered some money. But now it seems like they're going to put me in with all the rest of you minimum-wage gumshoes, no matter how good I am."

The argument was going better than expected, Frank thought as Joe made a fist, ready to strike. Audrey and Erin both appeared to be ready to step in as a small crowd of trainees gathered around them.

Frank tensed, but just as Joe pulled back his fist to punch his brother, the boys were interrupted by an angry male voice.

"All right, Agents Hill, pack your bags! You're both out of here on the next bus!"

Chapter

Four

"Sorry, Agent Banka," Frank said, backing off immediately. "We're just having a little disagreement." Frank had meant to draw attention, but not get kicked out! Mike Banka was a firearms instructor at the academy. Six foot two, Banka stood just a bit taller than Frank, and right then, furious, he seemed a lot bigger.

"I heard your 'disagreement,'" he snapped. "So did every recruit on campus. My advice to you is, if you don't like it here, get out or get some help."

"Yes, sir," Frank said sullenly, still playing the rebel.

"And as for money—there are plenty of opportunities in the bureau besides basic criminal chasing," Banka added brusquely. "If you want to talk them over with someone, see me in my office. But if I hear of any more scenes like this one, you're out. Is that understood?"

"Yes, sir," said the Hardys in unison.

"Good. Now go on to lunch," Banka added gruffly, "before I change my mind and put you on that bus now."

Erin and Audrey hung back to talk with Agent Banka. Frank thought Erin seemed uncomfortable.

"Way to go, Frank. We sure stirred something up there," Joe said as soon as they were out of earshot.

"Yeah, the question is, what?" Frank said. "That Banka's weird, don't you think? First threatening to kick me out, then suggesting I drop by his office to talk about money opportunities?"

"Sounds to me like he's either a very smart trainer, showing future agents how they can get ahead, or a recruiter for Autowatch," Joe agreed.

Frank nodded. "And he looks different from the other instructors, too. Not so straitlaced—like he doesn't think he has to conform to the FBI's clean-cut image."

"Which would make sense if someone else was paying him also," Joe pointed out. "I wonder why Audrey and Erin stayed to talk to him. You think they're reporting every word we said?"

Frank answered with a shrug. "Erin did seem really interested when I was talking about how I could make more money. Anyway, what do we know about Audrey and Erin so far?"

"Audrey's supposed to be brilliant in forensics," Joe replied. "That's why she joined the FBI. But she's terrible on the firing range."

"If she's worried about flunking out because she can't shoot, Banka might help her get through that," Frank responded. "If she supplies him with the right information."

"You could be right. She's definitely worth investigating some more," Joe said with a grin. "And I volunteer."

"Why am I not surprised?" Frank said. "In the meantime I'll try to find out more about Erin."

"They're worth checking out," Joe said, leading the way into the crowded, noisy cafeteria. "But right now, let's check out the food."

Nancy scanned the lunch crowd for Frank and Joe. She had heard their "argument" outside the lab and figured it was part of a plan to attract attention. Still, she knew Joe would never purposely miss a meal. Knowing that the Hardys were on campus made Nancy feel more secure. If she needed backup, they would be there—and backup didn't get any better.

Judy slipped into the seat next to hers. "Hey, we have the same lunch—a turkey sandwich and iced tea."

"I have to admit, the food here isn't bad," Nancy said. She glanced around the cafeteria. About a hundred NATS from all groups were grabbing quick meals before their next classes.

"I just called Agent Burr," Nancy told Judy. "Agent Havlicek did report the rope incident to him."

She felt Judy nudge her arm. "Here's someone you should meet," Judy said. She raised her arm and motioned to a fair-haired young woman who was carrying a tray, searching for a seat.

"Erin," Judy called, catching the agent's attention. The young woman approached their table. There were empty seats on either side of Nancy and Judy, but Erin remained standing.

"Nancy Douglas, this is Erin Seward, my roommate," Judy announced. "Erin, this is Nancy, a new trainee. Nancy's a French expert. *Parlez-vous français?*"

"No, I don't speak French," Erin said in an impatient tone, hardly glancing at Nancy. "I came with Audrey, but I've lost her. If you'll excuse me, I've got to look for her."

Erin took off almost immediately.

"She's not very friendly," Nancy commented, turning to Judy.

"She's okay. She just gets moody sometimes," Judy said.

Nancy nodded, but she couldn't help thinking that Erin's dislike of Judy was stronger than Judy realized. Nancy had met three agents—

Marianne, Jeff, and now Erin—and except for Jeff, none of them had been friendly to Judy or herself.

Nancy resolved to talk with Jeff Abelson later, to try to find out how well Judy really was liked.

After lunch Nancy and Judy rushed back to the dorm to change into the regulation dress for firearms practice: combat boots, canvas pants, T-shirt, and a navy blue baseball cap.

Nancy entered the range with mixed feelings. All forty trainees in her group were there. On the other side of a glass wall to her left, Nancy could see the rows of targets separated from one another by metal partitions. Nancy spotted a tall, dark-haired instructor and recognized him as the agent who had interrupted Frank and Joe outside the forensics lab.

"Hello, sir. I'm Nancy Douglas. I'm a new student," Nancy said, striding up to the instructor and extending her hand.

"Welcome to the academy, Agent Douglas," Mike Banka said, shaking Nancy's hand and eyeing her curiously. "I'm Agent Banka. I hope you'll enjoy our training sessions."

"Thank you, sir," Nancy replied.

"Training begins with ten minutes of individual practice with the red handles," Banka explained to her.

Nancy followed Banka down the hall to a counter where the other trainees were gathered.

Behind the counter Nancy could see an arsenal of weapons locked in a cage. This must be where Judy's attacker got the bullets, she realized.

"Agent LaFehr, front and center," Banka said, motioning forward a female agent with brown hair. "Audrey, this is Agent Nancy Douglas," Banka said. "Please explain the stance and sights to her after I give her a gun. I'll pass out your ammunition in a minute."

Banka unlocked the cabinet, selected a gun, and handed it to Nancy. It was slightly larger than her red handle. "This will be your training weapon. It's a Smith and Wesson Model Thirteen." He wrote the name *Douglas* on a piece of masking tape and attached it to the grip of the gun.

Nancy took the gun, noting how careful Banka had been to relock the cabinet. It would be difficult to steal bullets from the cabinets without that key, or without leaving some sign that there'd been a break-in. That meant that whoever shot Judy would have to be an agent with an already loaded gun, or a trainee who had miraculously managed to sneak out bullets during firearms class. Nancy's thoughts were interrupted by Banka's voice.

"Rule number one," he snapped, pulling the revolver back. "Never accept a weapon that isn't presented to you with the cylinder open and empty." Banka pulled the cylinder to the side, holding the unloaded weapon up for Nancy to inspect. "And I will not take this weapon back, Agent Douglas, unless you present it to me the same way. Understood?"

"Perfectly," Nancy replied, accepting the revolver from him.

Banka then handed her a pair of goggles and a set of protective earmuffs.

Nancy followed Audrey into the shooting area behind the glass wall.

"As you've probably gathered, I'm not an expert with guns." Audrey gave Nancy a rueful smile.

"That makes two of us," Nancy said easily.

"I'll stand behind you and help you with your stance, Audrey said. "Ready?" Nancy nodded. "Keep your legs about shoulders' width apart. Are you right-handed?"

"Yes," Nancy replied.

"Hold the gun in your right hand and extend your arm," Audrey said. Nancy obeyed.

"Now take your left hand and cup it under your right wrist. When you fire, this will help you keep the gun level." She explained how to hold the weapon, stand, and sight the target.

"Well, everything else is fairly simple. When Agent Banka is passing out rounds, the revolver is to be placed on this shelf, cylinder open," Audrey said, patting a small shelf.

"Banka brings out more rounds when new targets are set," Audrey continued, "so you have to open the gun again."

"You sound like you know what you're doing," Nancy said.

"I've got a great memory for facts," Audrey told her. "But I'm a lousy shot."

"After me, you'll probably look like Annie Oakley," Nancy said, laughing.

Banka appeared and passed out the rounds. Nancy put on the earmuffs Banka had given her and was struck by the quiet. It wouldn't last long. She had a feeling it would sound like a world war when the trainees started firing.

Audrey took her position in the stall next to Nancy's. When the target appeared she fired quickly. Then, just as quickly, she dropped her arms and shrieked. Nancy could clearly see the terror on the girl's face.

Nancy looked at Audrey's target. Tacked to it was a blown-up photo of Judy Noll!

Chapter

Five

"AUDREY, ARE YOU all right?" Nancy asked, yanking off her earmuffs. The photograph of Judy had three holes in the center of its smile. It sent a shiver up Nancy's spine.

Judy ran over to them. "Things are getting scary," she said.

Banka ordered everyone to stop firing. "What's the commotion here?" he asked Audrey and Nancy.

"Look at Audrey's target, sir," Nancy said.

Banka checked out the target, then turned to Judy. "It looks like somebody's playing games with you," he said to her.

"This is no game," Nancy said.

"Agent Noll, I want you to take that photograph and report to the administration offices," he ordered.

Judy nodded. "Can Agent Douglas come with me?" she asked. "I don't feel like going off by myself right now."

Banka frowned impatiently. "Agent Douglas has a lot of work to do on this range."

"I'll put in an extra hour of practice tomorrow," Nancy volunteered.

Banka hesitated. "I guess these are special circumstances," he said at last. "But I expect you to live up to your end of the bargain, Douglas."

"Yes, sir," Nancy replied.

As they left the range, Nancy asked if she recognized her picture.

"It's a copy of one that was taken when I graduated from college. I carry one in my purse to remind me that I can do anything if I put my mind to it," Judy said.

"Where do you usually keep your purse?" Nancy asked.

"In my room during firearms training," Judy said.

"What about the rest of the day?" Nancy asked.

"Well, I keep it in my locker during PE, and I take it with me to lectures and lunch," Judy said. "Why? What are you thinking?"

"Someone must have taken that photograph out of your purse and had it enlarged," Nancy

39

A Nancy Drew & Hardy Boys SuperMystery

replied. "If we can figure out who had access to your purse, we may have a clue to who's after you."

"It could have been anyone; there aren't any locks on our doors at the dorm."

"When did you see the photo last?" Nancy asked.

"The last time I remember seeing it was when I first got to the academy."

As she and Judy crossed the central square, Nancy heard Judy say in a low voice, "I don't know how much more of this I can take."

Nancy thought out loud. "Maybe that's what your attacker wants," she said. "Think about it. Those shots missed you by a healthy margin— about seven feet, I think the report said. Then we have no proof that rope trick *was* aimed at you this morning. And that poster on the target just now was just a scare tactic."

"But what could it all mean?" Judy asked curiously.

Nancy shrugged. "It's possible that whoever's doing this doesn't want to hurt you, they just want you to leave the academy."

"But who?" Judy said.

"I'm not sure," Nancy said. She was quiet for a few moments, thinking about what she knew of the agents she'd met so far. "Tell me more about Marianne Risi," she said.

"Well—Marianne's about the most competitive student here. Next week the NATS will get ranked in every subject. The people with the highest rankings at the end of the course get the top assignments. Marianne keeps bragging about how she's going to be number one. I hate to brag myself, but I am probably her toughest competition."

"I wonder how far she'd go to be number one," Nancy wondered out loud.

Nancy and Judy entered the administration building and took the elevator to the third floor. A man in his early thirties was sitting at a desk outside Burr's office.

"Is Agent Burr in?" Nancy asked him.

"No, he's in the field," the man replied. "I'm Agent Kane. Can I help?"

Judy explained what had happened on the range, and she and Nancy spent the next hour telling Agent Kane their stories. Then he filled out what seemed like a hundred forms for another hour. When they finally finished, Nancy and Judy headed back to the dorm.

"What's on the agenda for the rest of the day?" Nancy asked.

"Firearms practice lasts until five, and then supper. We're free until lights out at ten o'clock. I usually go jogging in the woods after dinner. It's really peaceful. We could go now."

"Do you think it's a good idea to run in the woods when someone may be stalking you?" Nancy asked.

"With two of us, I'd feel safe. A fit body leads to a fit mind—or at least that's what they say around here," Judy said.

41

"Okay, you win," Nancy said, shaking her head in amazement. "You are the most determined bunch of people I've ever met."

Nancy had to admit she did feel refreshed after their run and a quick shower. She and Judy ate supper with the rest of the trainees, then went on to the library to study. Nancy used her time to catch up on some of the fingerprinting techniques she had missed learning about.

"I'm exhausted," Nancy told Judy as they walked back from the library to the dorm.

"The bureau makes it tough on purpose," Judy explained. "It's a weeding-out process." She fixed her determined blue eyes on Nancy. "That's part of the reason I decided not to drop out. I've never been beaten before, and I'm not about to be now."

Nancy wearily climbed the stairs that led to their rooms on the second floor. She heard animated voices from the lounge at the top of the stairs. She checked her watch. It read 9:45.

"Hi, Judy. Hi, Nancy," she heard Audrey call out. Nancy poked her head into the lounge to see Audrey sitting next to Erin Seward on a brown vinyl couch. Audrey gave Nancy a shy smile— obviously the dark-haired trainee had recovered from her experience at the firing range. Nancy noticed that Erin focused her eyes on her book as soon as Judy came into the lounge. Nancy also noticed Jeff Abelson sitting in a chair next to Audrey and Erin.

"Nancy!" Jeff said, breaking into a wide grin. He was dressed in jeans and a green polo shirt that matched his eyes. Nancy thought he looked even cuter than he had in the gym—and just as friendly. "I missed you at dinner."

"Well, if it isn't Miss Accident Prone and her new best friend," Marianne said, interrupting Jeff and Nancy.

"How are you, Marianne?" Nancy asked politely.

"A lot better off than Agent Noll here," Marianne replied. "Judy, it sure seems as though somebody's out to get you. I hope that doesn't get you kicked out of the program."

"You don't have any ideas about who could be after her, do you?" Nancy asked dryly.

Marianne shrugged, perched on the edge of one of the couches. "Right now I'm sick of hearing about poor Judy. Just because she's a senator's kid, she gets all this extra attention."

"That's not true and you know it, Marianne," Judy retorted. "And why should I be ashamed because my father's a success?"

"Hey, break it up," Jeff said, laughing uncomfortably.

"You tell her to break it up, Agent Abelson," Judy snapped. "Marianne's jealous. Jealous because I'm beating her and jealous because I'm rich, too."

"Right, Noll," Marianne snapped. "You always have all the answers." She turned to Nancy. "Speaking of answers, I have a question for you.

43

How did you get accepted into this program so late?"

Nancy heard the note of suspicion in Marianne's voice and told her about her French degree and having volunteered for a special FBI mission.

From her perch on the sofa, Marianne looked thoughtful. "You look pretty young to have a master's degree in French," she said. "What did you do, skip some years in high school?"

"Well, y-yes," Nancy stammered, turning away from Jeff. "And I made it through college fast, too."

"I speak French," Audrey said with a smile. "Maybe we could practice together."

"That would be great," Nancy said. Silently she prayed it would never happen.

Just then, the group heard footsteps coming up the stairs. Judy called out, "Frank! Joe! You guys are back late!"

The Hardys stepped into the lounge. "Hi, Judy," Frank said. "We just finished in the library. I don't know about you, but we're beat."

Frank caught Nancy's eye, and she guessed he needed to talk to her.

"I'll be back in a minute," she murmured to Judy. "I need to get something from my room."

Nancy started down the hallway, relieved to get away from her questioners. Behind her she heard Joe talking to Judy and the others, diverting their attention so Frank could slip away.

A moment later Frank joined Nancy outside her room.

"I wanted to talk to you at the shooting range today, but you and Judy left in a hurry," Frank said breathlessly.

"What happened was pretty scary," Nancy said, happy to be able to share her feelings openly with someone. "My case is getting more puzzling. How's yours going?"

"Not great, but we have a few tentative suspects," Frank said. "That's why I wanted to talk to you. One of them is Audrey LaFehr. She's in danger of flunking out because she's a lousy shot," Frank said. "And that puts her at the top of our list."

"If Audrey's your suspect, then Mike Banka could well be her recruiter," she agreed excitedly. "He's the one with the power to pass or fail Audrey in firearms."

"Right," Frank said. "It's not much, but it's all we've got to go on." He hesitated. "I was wondering about Erin Seward, too. She seemed interested one time when I brought up the subject of money."

"I have some suspicions about Erin," Nancy said grimly. "I'll tell you about them later."

"Fine. Listen, I was wondering," Frank said, hesitating. "I know it's not your case and all, but since you're Audrey's firearms partner, do you think you could keep your eyes open for me?"

"No problem," Nancy said, and smiled.

"Thanks. You're the best," Frank said warmly.

"We'd better get back to the lounge before anyone notices we're both gone," Nancy murmured.

"It's too late for that." Nancy whirled around to see Jeff Abelson standing in the hallway a few feet away.

"Jeff!" Nancy wondered if the trainee had heard more than he was supposed to. "Frank was just offering to tutor me on the material I've missed so far," Nancy said, thinking quickly.

Jeff moved closer, putting an arm around Nancy's shoulders. "Sounds like a good idea. You wouldn't happen to need two tutors, would you, Agent Douglas?" he teased cheerfully.

"We'll see about that," she said, ducking out from under Jeff's arm. Then she pretended to yawn and stretch. "It's lights out, you guys. I'm going to bed."

"Good idea," Frank said.

Nancy entered her room and closed her door behind her. Jeff was so cute! She was almost positive he was only trying to flirt with her, but he could be dangerous, she reminded herself. Until this thing was solved, everyone had to be under suspicion. Nancy sighed. Sometimes it was hard to remember she was a detective, and not just a normal teenage girl.

* * *

Joe Hardy jumped as the hoot of an owl pierced the night air. "Frank? Is that you?" he called softly.

"That was just an owl, Joe," his brother replied. Frank was crouched behind a bush about ten feet from Joe. Joe didn't understand why they had to risk getting caught out after lights out, but Frank had convinced him that if the Autowatch recruiter wanted to line up a student or two, he would probably make contact after hours. So the boys had sneaked out of their room and positioned themselves about twenty feet from the front doors of the dorm. It was humid and hot, even this late at night, but Frank felt if they could catch the recruiter in action, the discomfort would be worth it.

"Frank, it's almost midnight," Joe said in a hoarse whisper. "Don't you think we should go back inside?"

"Just a few more minutes, Joe," Frank said.

Joe crouched back down behind his bush just as a dark sedan pulled up in the parking lot next to the dorm.

A few seconds later the front door opened, and a slim woman with long blond hair came out, clutching a large envelope. It was too dark to see her face, but for a moment Joe thought that it could be Nancy. That was ridiculous, he knew.

The person in the car turned on the headlights. Joe couldn't make out the driver's face, but he could tell that it was a man. He turned back to the young woman. For a brief instant her face was illuminated in the headlights as she made her way around the front of the car. Joe stifled a gasp. It was Erin Seward handing the envelope to the driver!

Chapter

Six

"ERIN!" JOE WHISPERED as the young woman turned and disappeared back into the dorm. "I knew Audrey was innocent. Let's go, Frank!" He took off like a shot after the car as it pulled out of the lot.

"Have to get that license number," Joe mumbled. The car's taillights barely illuminated the plate, and Joe was able to make out only the first three figures as the sedan sped away.

"Did you get anything, Joe?" Frank asked, appearing beside his brother.

Joe shook his head. "Not much. Just the first three digits. Seven U-N."

"That may be enough," Frank said. "The plate

was white with blue letters, right? Those are the colors of Washington, D.C., plates. If we give what we have to the Network, they should be able to give us a list of names of car owners in D.C. whose plates begin with seven U-N. That sedan was definitely a foreign make. That should narrow the list even further."

Still, there was so much that puzzled Joe. "Frank, what exactly did we witness out here tonight?"

"What do you mean?" his brother asked.

"If Erin was meeting a recruiter, why was *she* giving *him* an envelope? If she's getting paid, shouldn't it be the other way around?"

Frank became thoughtful. "That's a good point. Maybe she was giving him some kind of information. Actually, what bugs me is that it was Erin Seward out here. I was sure it had to be Audrey and Banka."

Joe shook his head. "I know you think I'm just infatuated with her," he protested, "but every instinct I have says Audrey isn't our suspect. Even if she is vulnerable, I just don't think she has it in her to turn against the bureau." He thought of Banka and something clicked. "But wait a minute," he said excitedly. "That man in the car was big, wasn't he? Maybe it was Banka!"

"All we have to do to find out for sure is check out his car."

"Let's do it tomorrow. I don't even want to know what time it is," Joe said wearily.

"I'm with you. This training schedule is lethal," Frank agreed as they stole back into the darkened dorm.

Nancy Drew lay in bed, watching her roommate sleep peacefully. I wish I could sleep, too, Nancy thought. I definitely need my rest.

Still, she couldn't turn her mind off and stop going over the case in her head. First there was the shooting. Who had had the opportunity to shoot at Judy? Judy had told Nancy that Erin was the only person who knew Judy wasn't attending the lecture. Even so, anyone could have found that out. Could that anyone be Jeff? Nancy wondered. He had left the lecture just a few minutes before Judy was shot at. Ever since Nancy had arrived, it seemed, he'd been hanging around her. Maybe he suspected something and was trying to find out who she really was.

Then there was the rope incident. When would anyone have been able to cut the rope? The gym opened at six A.M. so trainees could put in extra PT. Nancy glanced at Marianne again. Hadn't Marianne said she liked to train early? She had left their room very early that morning, and could have cut the rope before other people showed up. But how could anyone know Judy would use that rope?

Judy's photo on the target, Nancy thought. Who had access to the photo in Judy's purse? Erin would have had the best opportunity, but that didn't mean that Jeff, Marianne, or anyone else couldn't have stolen it.

Then there was Banka, who had access to both the bullets and the targets. Where did Judy's father, the senator, fit into all this? Nancy had to admit she hadn't given much thought to Judy's father yet. She'd have to find out more about him.

What I really need, Nancy decided, is to take a close look at these people's records. Burr had said she could be excused from classes once or twice if she felt Judy was safe for the time. I'll call him first thing in the morning, Nancy thought. She punched her pillow and closed her eyes, determined to get some sleep.

Nancy had barely closed her eyes when she heard the soft thud of footsteps in the hallway outside her door. Instantly alert, she climbed out of bed, tiptoed across the room, and pulled the door open a crack.

She cringed as it let out a high-pitched creak. Nancy glanced quickly over at Marianne, who still appeared to be sleeping peacefully. Nancy breathed a sigh of relief, then turned her attention to the hallway.

A few doors down, Nancy saw Erin Seward entering the room she shared with Judy. Even in the dim light, Nancy could see that Erin's face looked flushed, maybe from fear or excitement.

What on earth was Erin doing up at this hour? Nancy wondered as she quickly pulled her head back out of sight. It was after midnight!

Nancy started to pull her door closed, but then she heard more sounds. The echo of footsteps and low voices on the stairwell near the lounge stopped her.

Nancy took a deep breath, then slipped out into the hall. Staying close to the wall, she made her way down the hall to the stairwell. The voices were coming from the stairs. It sounded like two men.

Moving toward the door that separated the stairwell from the second-floor hallway, Nancy held her breath.

Just as she reached out to touch the doorknob, a floorboard beneath Nancy's foot creaked loudly. She froze, her heart pounding, listening to the sudden silence in the stairwell.

Then the door flew open.

"Frank!" she whispered, just stopping herself from screaming. Nancy whispered, "What are you two doing sneaking around up here?"

"Sorry, Nancy. But I guess we could ask you the same thing," Frank said.

"Trying to protect my client, of course," Nancy whispered.

Joe yawned. "I'll let you guys chat without me. I'm beat," he said, disappearing up the stairs to the third floor.

"Wait a minute," Nancy said to Frank, leading him into the dark, empty lounge, where they could whisper without disturbing anyone. She closed the door and turned to face Frank in the moonlit room. "Does your being here have anything to do with the fact that I just saw Erin Seward sneaking into her room?" she asked.

"Sort of," Frank began. Nancy listened as Frank filled her in on what he and Joe had seen outside. "We're not sure what we just saw, and I don't want to make any assumptions. There are too many loose ends," he said. "For one thing, I can't understand why Erin would be giving a recruiter an envelope—if he *was* a recruiter."

"That is a little strange," Nancy agreed. "But I know what you mean about loose ends. Burr said Judy got along well with the other trainees here, but nearly everyone I've met seems to have a grudge against her. Still, Judy herself doesn't have a clue as to who might want to hurt her, and apparently her father doesn't, either.

"I feel like my case is full of *mights* and *maybes,* too," Nancy continued. "Marianne *might* have cut that rope. Erin *might* have taken that photo out of Judy's purse and had it blown up. Jeff *might* have left the lecture because he knew Judy was alone in her room."

"Are you sure you don't want me to protect you from Jeff, Nancy?" Frank interrupted. "He sure seems to be after you. He may distract you from your case."

Nancy knew from the smile on Frank's face that he was teasing her. "He may be cute, but he's not cute enough to make me blow this case," Nancy said.

"I don't know. He could get persistent," Frank said.

"I can handle myself with Jeff," Nancy said. "Besides, you know I wouldn't do anything to hurt Ned."

"I know," Frank said. Ned Nickerson was Nancy's boyfriend back home in River Heights. Frank and Nancy had been attracted to each other when they'd worked on other cases. It was Nancy's loyalty to Ned and Frank's loyalty to his girlfriend, Callie Shaw, that had kept them apart.

Nancy quickly changed the subject. "There is something you and Joe can do for me, Frank. I'm going to see if Burr can get me excused from PT tomorrow so I can look through some of the trainees' files. Can you keep an eye on Judy for me during class? After what happened yesterday, I'd hate to leave her alone."

"Sure thing, Nancy. Just keep your eyes open for anything interesting about Audrey LaFehr. I'm still convinced she's involved somehow."

"No problem," Nancy said. "Even if I do agree with Joe that she seems pretty nice." She couldn't help yawning. "Speaking of Joe, I think he had the right idea. We'd better get some sleep."

"Okay," Frank said. "I'll go out first, then you. It's quieter that way."

Frank slipped out of the lounge and up the flight of stairs. Nancy waited for a moment, then she, too, stole out of the lounge.

There were no windows in the corridor, and

the only light came from the moonlit lounge. Nancy could hardly see her hand in front of her face as she moved down the hall.

She had only taken two small steps when a pair of hands reached out from the darkness and grabbed her arms, pinning them to her sides.

"I knew I'd catch you sneaking around!" a voice growled in the darkness.

Nancy drew her breath in with a gasp. The hands gripping her hurt. In the faint moonlight, she made out the face of Marianne Risi. Her dark eyes were blazing.

"I'm not sure what you and Frank were up to, Nancy," Marianne snarled. "But when I find out, you better believe I'll use it to get you thrown out!"

Chapter

Seven

DON'T PANIC, Nancy told herself. There's got to be a way out of this. "Frank and I were just talking," she said. "We're friends."

"Oh, really?" Marianne said, raising an eyebrow. "You and Judy are friends, too, but I don't see you meeting *her* secretly after hours."

This isn't going to be easy, Nancy thought. "All right, Marianne, I should have known I couldn't keep a secret from someone like you."

"What kind of secret?" Marianne asked.

"If you must know, Frank Hill and I—well, we like each other," Nancy confessed, trying to appear embarrassed. "The daily routine here is so busy that we thought we would try to sneak out."

"Well, isn't that sweet," Marianne said snidely. "I'm not sure if I believe you, Douglas."

"It's the truth," Nancy protested nervously. "I met Frank and Joe years ago, when we were all counselors at a children's summer camp. Now that we've run into each other again, I don't know—" she sighed, sounding lovesick. "Something clicked, I guess. We just had to talk it out."

"Hmm. A likely story," Marianne said. Nancy thought that she believed it, though.

"Can we keep this between us?" Nancy pleaded.

"I'll think about it, Douglas," Marianne said. "Right now I want to get to sleep."

A short while later Nancy was listening to Marianne's light, steady breathing. She yawned, hoping Frank wouldn't mind the story she concocted.

At exactly six the next morning, Nancy awoke to the steady beeping of her digital alarm clock. Fumbling for the button, she glanced across the room. Marianne was already gone.

Pulling on her bathrobe, Nancy walked to the pay phone at the end of the hall. A few of the other agents were awake and heading for the showers. Making sure no one was in earshot, Nancy punched in the numbers Agent Burr had given her.

"Yes, Nancy, my assistant contacted me about yesterday's incident with the photograph," said Burr's gravelly voice. "It's unlikely that the enlargement was done on campus, but we're checking."

Burr was less than eager to let Nancy be excused from PT in order to go through trainee files. "You're a bodyguard, Nancy, not a detective. You stick close to Judy."

"But, Agent Burr," Nancy murmured, careful not to be overheard, "so far, your agents have turned up nothing, and Judy's still being attacked. I'm getting to know the trainees here, and I've come up with questions that your agents wouldn't think to ask. Just give me a few hours with the files."

Finally Agent Burr agreed. Nancy hung up quickly and ran to get dressed.

At breakfast Nancy quickly told Judy about her plans for the morning. "I hate to leave you alone, but I have some leads to check out," she said.

"If you say so, Nancy," Judy said. "I'll be glad when PT's over, though."

"Who isn't glad when PT's over?" Nancy kidded. Deep down, she was worried about leaving Judy, but knowing that Frank and Joe would keep an eye on her made Nancy feel a little better.

Nancy made her way across the campus to the administration building in the hot summer sun.

"Hello, Agent Douglas," Burr said as Nancy entered his office. "I told Agent Havlicek that I needed you to translate some documents for me, but I'm afraid I can't excuse you from your criminal law class."

The offices were so quiet, it was spooky, Nancy thought. Only the hum of a copy machine and the occasional telephone ring kept the place from being as quiet as a tomb. Burr led her down a corridor to a small room. "I had the files pulled of all the NATS, including Judy's." He set a pile of folders on a metal desk.

"Good luck," he added grudgingly. "I'll have someone call you when it's almost ten o'clock." As soon as Burr left, Nancy opened Marianne's file.

What Nancy read surprised her. Marianne had been a physical education major in college and joined the local police force after graduation. Nancy knew that many NATS were former police officers, but she had a hard time picturing Marianne doing some of the friendlier things that police officers did—like helping kids cross the street. In fact, Nancy couldn't picture Marianne being nice to anyone.

Erin Seward was from a small farm community in Iowa. Erin's mother had died when she was a baby, and her father died when she was only thirteen. Left penniless, Erin, an only child, was sent to live with an aunt. She graduated from high school with honors and attended college on a scholarship, where she studied history and computer science. She had intended to go to law school, but wasn't able to get financial aid. Instead, she became a computer operator and applied to the FBI after three years in the field.

Nancy thought. No wonder Frank had said money interested Erin—her life had certainly been affected by the lack of it.

Judy's file contrasted sharply with Erin's, and included a few facts that Agent Burr hadn't mentioned to Nancy earlier. Reading the file, Nancy learned that Judy had been an only child whose mother had died when she was young. Even back then, though, Judy's father had been very wealthy. As he climbed the political ladder and grew increasingly powerful, Judy attended private schools, an Ivy League college, and finally one of the country's top law schools.

Nancy did notice that Judy's grades in college were mostly Bs and Cs—not the grades one would need to get into an important law school. Suddenly Nancy wondered whether being the daughter of a senator really had had something to do with Judy's admission.

Judy had achieved everything Erin had ever dreamed of, even though she might not have earned it.

No wonder Erin reacted coolly to Judy, Nancy thought. But could Erin resent her roommate enough to hurt or kill her?

There was nothing disturbing in Audrey LaFehr's file, Nancy noted. A brilliant computer science student, Audrey had applied to the bureau after she received her master's degree. According to her personal profile, Audrey's dream was to bring her knowledge and experience to the sophisticated systems used by the FBI.

Jeff Abelson's file revealed someone destined to become a special agent: his grandfather, father, and two older brothers were all members or former members of the bureau. Jeff had spent two years with a top accounting firm before being accepted into the academy. Nancy knew that the bureau always needed accountants. After all, it was an accountant who had put Al Capone away.

Nancy was deep in thought when an assistant appeared to tell her it was time for her next class. Nancy thanked her and reluctantly left the room. She wished she had more time.

That's okay, she thought as she hurried out the door. She knew from previous cases that something that didn't seem important at first could later provide the key to a solution. With any luck, she had come across one of those keys that morning.

"Frank, I'm all for cutting class, but are you sure we won't get kicked out for it?" Joe asked as he followed his brother out of the gym.

"Not for skipping just one class," Frank said. "Besides, with any luck, we'll find out the information we need to close this case. Then we won't have to worry about any more classes."

"We have to check out two things," Frank continued as they made their way toward the parking lot. "First, the license number of Banka's car. Second, if it's not the one we're looking for, we need to find out how an outside car could get onto the academy grounds." The Network had provided Frank and his brother with a compact car for this case, and the Hardys had had to purchase a special ID sticker to park on campus. They knew that a manned security station checked all other incoming vehicles twenty-four hours a day.

"How are we supposed to find all this out?" Joe asked.

"We'll ask. That usually works," Frank said as they approached the small concrete security building.

"I'm Agent Hill," Frank said, offering his hand to the gray-haired man behind the station. "This is my brother, Joe. We were wondering if you could answer a question for us."

The older man squinted through his wire-rimmed glasses. "That depends on the question, young man."

Frank flashed a friendly smile. "Our father was planning to visit us this weekend. He's bringing some workout equipment from home," Frank improvised.

Joe took up the story. "We were wondering if he'd be allowed to drive up to the dorm. Does he need a special pass or anything?"

"He needs to fill out this twenty-four-hour pass application." The man pulled a piece of paper out of a drawer in front of him. "Then he shows up with two forms of ID and it's done.

Frank took the paper from him. "Sounds simple enough," he said, still smiling. "Tell me, does the academy get a lot of visitors?"

"Oh, sure." The man chuckled. "Believe me, this job keeps me on my toes."

"Thanks for the application. We'll bring it back later," Joe said. He turned his head toward the nearby parking area reserved for academy instructors. "That sure is a nice set of wheels," he said, pointing to a shiny red convertible. "Isn't that Agent Banka's car?"

"No, that's Samantha Havlicek's," the man said. He nodded toward a dark blue car farther down the lot. "See that sedan down there? That's Banka's car."

Frank tried not to reveal his excitement. It was the same model as the car they had seen the night before.

"I can't believe it," Joe said as he caught up to his brother. "This could be our big break."

"I hope so, Joe," Frank said. His excitement grew—until the license plate came in view.

"Eight A-X, seven-six-four," Frank read aloud. "It looks like it wasn't Banka last night."

Frank led his brother out of the parking area and continued along under the shade of the adjoining woods. Their walk back to their classroom was quiet. Frank kept running the events of the night before over in his mind. He supposed Joe was doing the same.

Suddenly the silence was broken by the sharp snap of a tree branch.

"Did you hear that?" Frank whispered. "We're being followed."

Frank heard another snap and turned just in time to see a figure slipping out of the woods.

It was Mike Banka!

Chapter

Eight

"Let's get him!" Joe said as Banka turned and ran.

"Wait." Joe felt Frank grip his arm. "What reason do we have to grab him?"

"He was spying on us!" Joe answered.

"If we chase him, we risk blowing our cover," Frank pointed out. "We know where to find him. The question is, why was he spying? Maybe we're getting close to something," he continued excitedly. "Remember when Banka asked us to come to his office for a talk? Maybe he really is the Autowatch recruiter—even if his car isn't the one we saw last night—and he's thinking about recruiting us."

"He has a funny way of doing it," Joe grumbled. "A simple invitation would do the job."

Back in the cafeteria Joe stared approvingly at the ham sandwich and potato salad on his lunch tray. He joined Frank and Nancy at a table. The two of them were already comparing notes.

"So you think Banka was spying on you?" Nancy said to Frank.

"I really think we could be onto something," Frank insisted. "He could be our man."

"Pipe down, you two," Joe scolded. A group of NATS were sitting at a table just a few feet away. Marianne was one of them, and Joe noticed her looking at Frank with interest.

"Sorry," Frank said, lowering his voice. "By the way, where's Judy?"

"She's having lunch with her father off campus," Nancy replied. "Thanks for looking out for her during PT," she added. "I talked to her in criminal law class, and she told me nothing scary happened."

"Right," Frank said. "If you don't count Audrey."

"Audrey?" Nancy asked, interested.

Joe made a face. "Frank thinks it's hilarious that Audrey flipped me on my back a few times during our martial arts workout."

Nancy stared at Joe. "Audrey flipped you?"

Joe flushed. "Look, Nancy, she may be short, but she happens to be a brown belt, okay?"

Nancy hooted with laughter until Frank, feeling sorry for his brother, changed the subject. "I'm surprised no one gave Judy a hard time about having lunch off campus," he said.

"Having the lunch with her father the senator probably doesn't hurt," Joe said.

"From what I read in her files, having a father for a senator has helped Judy in plenty of ways," Nancy said. "Although it may be unfair to blame Judy for that."

"Did you find anything that might help us?" Frank asked Nancy, leaning forward to hear her above the din of the mealtime chatter.

Quickly she told the Hardys what she had read about Erin.

"That's great, Nancy. Erin fits the Autowatch profile perfectly," Frank said.

"She's definitely at the top of our suspect list," Joe agreed. "She couldn't have made that midnight rendezvous for any innocent reason."

"Don't forget about Audrey, though," Nancy added. "I mean, I think she's really nice, but we've all had the wool pulled over our eyes before."

"Especially him," Frank said, motioning toward Joe. "Whenever there's a pretty girl around, he loses his objectivity."

Joe scowled as Frank and Nancy burst out laughing. "Get off my case, you guys," he said. "Audrey's being cute has nothing to do with why I think she's innocent. Her file proves she's way too smart to get involved with the Autowatch scam."

"You have a point, little brother," Frank said.

"Hey, Frank!" Nancy and the Hardys looked up to see Marianne calling to them over the roar of cafeteria conversation. "Where were you and Joe during criminal law class?"

"We were, um, helping Hoffman set up the fingerprint-detecting apparatus for the next forensics class," Joe answered quickly for his brother. "He gave us a pass—that is, if it's any business of yours."

Marianne shrugged. "They usually kick you out if you skip a class with no excuse."

"Right," Frank shouted. "Thanks for your concern, Agent Risi."

"That reminds me," Nancy said in a low voice to Frank after Marianne had turned away. "Marianne caught us talking last night. I'm not sure exactly what she saw—or heard. I made up a story about our sneaking off to be alone," Nancy said, batting her eyelashes at Frank. "Two young agents on a romantic rendezvous. I think she bought it."

"Good thinking, sweetheart," Frank said with a grin. "From now on, if we get caught talking over our cases in a hidden corner somewhere, I'll say that I'm whispering sweet nothings in your ear."

"I can't believe this," Joe said. "Not to change the subject, but what's our game plan for the rest of the day?"

"Personally, I'm stumped," Nancy said, stabbing at her salad with a fork. "So while I wait for Judy's attacker to give him- or herself away, I'll keep an eye on Audrey for you. We're teamed up on the firing range this afternoon."

"Thanks," Frank said. "That way, Joe and I can concentrate on Erin."

"And Banka," Joe added. "I'm anxious to see how the mad peeper acts around us."

"If you guys really think he might try to recruit you," Nancy pointed out, "another argument like yesterday's might convince him to make his move."

"Good thinking," Frank agreed. "If we do it at the range, we'll be able to feel out Banka, Erin, and Audrey all at once."

"Time to stop eating and start investigating," Nancy said, leaning closer to Joe. "Look who's headed our way."

Joe and Frank turned to see Erin Seward walking toward their table.

As Erin got closer, Joe could see why he had mistaken her for Nancy the night before. Today they were both wearing their reddish blond hair loose. Erin's was turned up slightly at her shoulders, and Joe could see that her eyes were green, not blue like Nancy's, but otherwise they could be cousins.

"Hi, guys," Erin said a bit nervously. "Where's Judy?"

"She's having lunch with her father," Nancy told her. "Why don't you join us? Did you finish eating?"

"I already ate," Erin said. She sat next to

Frank. "You two aren't fighting again, are you?" she said to Joe.

"Why do you ask?" Joe responded. "Did you want to take Frank's side?"

"I do understand Frank's point about money. Life isn't easy if you don't have enough of it. That I know for sure." She paused and stared down at the table.

"That's my point exactly," Frank said, watching her carefully. "No one's going to look out for you if you don't look out for yourself."

Erin nodded, frowning. "There's another side to that story, though," she said. "When it comes down to it, money isn't the most important consideration. I mean, working for a big corporation's fine if money's all you want. But it's who you are and what you do that counts to me. I really believe that. I guess that's why I'm here," Erin said, blushing slightly.

"I'm babbling," she said. "I just wanted to tell you, Frank, that I'm glad you're sticking with the bureau, too. Well, I'll see you around." She abruptly stood and left the table.

"What was that all about?" Frank asked.

"Either she really means what she just said," Joe said, "or she's trying to throw us off the scent."

"I think she meant what she said," Frank admitted. "Maybe she's not guilty after all."

"Now who's trusting his hormones instead of his head?" Joe asked. "Just a few minutes ago you said she was guilty. Now that she tells you you're a great guy for staying—"

Nancy interrupted them. "It's almost time for target practice. I have to meet Judy back at the dorm. Let's go for a jog after supper," she suggested. "We can compare notes again then. I'll have to bring Judy, though. After all, I am her bodyguard."

"No sweat," Joe said. "I'll distract her."

When Joe and Frank arrived on the range, some of the other NATS had already begun red handle practice.

Banka's whistle blew, and the NATS lined up to receive the weapons that had been assigned to them. It was Joe and Frank's signal to begin their second argument over money.

"Serving your country is fine," Frank grumbled as the brothers moved closer to the counter, "but you also have to look out for number one."

"Dad would be ashamed of you," Joe admonished, raising his voice enough for Banka, who was distributing the weapons, to hear. "This isn't about a paycheck. It's about helping your fellow man. It's not fair. I have so much trouble passing these classes, and they're all easy for you. And all you care about is making big bucks!"

"You two just don't listen, do you?"

Joe raised his eyes to see Banka glaring at them

from behind the counter. Out of the corner of his eye, Joe noted that both Erin and Audrey were watching them.

Banka passed Frank the shotgun with his name taped to the stock. Joe was given a shotgun, too. Joe recognized the Remington Standard Model 870s they'd been assigned the past week. They had shot with them only once before.

"I'm not going to tell you two again," Banka said tersely. "Any more talk like this and you can both drive off to the city and try to get some corporation to hire you."

"Sorry, sir," Joe replied. "It's my brother. He's just—"

"I don't care what he is," Banka shouted. "Just can it."

Intrigued by how angry their instructor had become, Joe and Frank moved away with their weapons. Banka, red-faced, handed the last few trainees their guns. Then he shouted, "Everyone file outside to the range."

Joe moved past Erin and Audrey, who seemed to have lost interest in the Hardys. So much for that experiment, he thought, exiting the building.

As Joe followed the others outside, he eyed the twenty targets curiously. They were shaped like people and were life-size.

"Why'd Banka get so angry when he overheard us?" Joe whispered to his brother. He shifted the light shotgun in his arms.

"Who knows?" Frank replied. "At least we got

a reaction from him. We know he's paying attention."

Joe checked out the crowd of trainees. Nancy stood at the far end of the target range with Judy, talking with Audrey and Jeff. Erin stood with Marianne as they compared earmuffs. Joe noted that some of the NATS were carrying Remington shotguns like his and Frank's, and others had Smith & Wesson Model 13 revolvers.

"The group with the Remingtons will fire at the targets on the east end of the range," Banka said, joining them. "Those with revolvers will fire at the west end. As you all know, it's important to learn to use the revolver before you move on to a shotgun."

Joe noticed that Nancy and Audrey both had revolvers as they moved toward the targets nearest them.

Joe and Frank's group moved toward the east end of the range and donned their protective gear while waiting for Banka to issue their envelopes of ammunition. "I'm going to beat you today," Joe said to Frank before he put on his earmuffs.

"Uh-huh. Dream on," Frank said.

The targets beckoned down the length of the dirt field. Joe guessed they must be some thirty yards away. He accepted the envelope of shells that Banka handed him, loaded the Remington, then trained the sights on the outline of a man in front of him. He aimed for the heart, sure he could score in the kill zone and show Frank up. He turned to his brother, hoping to get in one last insult, but the sound of an unusually loud explosion stopped him cold.

The barrel of Frank's gun was black and twisted, and Joe watched as his brother toppled backward in eerie slow motion.

Frank's gun had backfired!

Chapter

Nine

"Frank, ARE YOU all right?" Frank barely heard
his brother's voice through the loud ringing in his
ears.

Frank sat upright on the cold ground and took
off his earmuffs. A white light clouded his eyes,
and his hands felt sore and burned. He thought
about standing, but somehow that didn't seem
like a great idea.

"Frank, talk to me!" Frank's vision began to
clear. He made out Joe's face. Several other
NATS, including Nancy, Judy, and Jeff, had
gathered around him, too. Banka was running
toward them.

"What happened, Frank?" Nancy asked,
kneeling down next to him.

76

"I'm not sure," Frank replied. "There was just—a big explosion."

Nancy and Joe helped Frank to stand. Frank grabbed their shoulders for support and winced as his hands made contact. Checking his hands, he was shocked at how raw and red his palms were.

Frank saw that Banka had picked up his shotgun. "It's obvious what happened here," the instructor said in disgust. He pointed to the barrel, which seemed to have split open. Black gunk oozed out of the ragged opening. "The shell couldn't get past the dirt in your barrel. I showed you how to clean this rifle after you shot it last week. Obviously you weren't paying attention."

Banka studied Frank's hands. "You're a lucky man, Hill. Your hands are going to be sore for a while, and your body's going to ache from the impact. But if this barrel had been clogged shut, I guarantee the explosion would have been a lot worse."

"But, sir," Frank said, "I'm positive I cleaned that barrel last week!"

Banka ignored him. "Everyone back to your stations!" he ordered. "We're going to carry out a thorough inspection before another shot is fired. Joe, take your brother to the infirmary. He needs to get those hands checked out."

Frank found that he needed to lean on Joe as they walked out. His legs still felt unsteady. "I know I cleaned my rifle last week," he said when they were out of earshot. "Someone jammed it deliberately."

Joe nodded grimly. "I know, Frank. And we both know the one person who had the perfect opportunity to do it," he said, pointing at Banka.

I hope Frank's all right, Nancy thought as she changed into her gray sweats. She hadn't seen either of the Hardys at dinner. She eyed her digital clock. She still had a few minutes before she had to meet them on the jogging trail in the woods.

Nancy glanced at the items neatly arranged on Marianne's dresser. She knew her roommate was working out in the weight room. This would be the perfect time to check for any incriminating evidence. Until now Marianne's aggressive behavior had been enough to make Nancy suspicious of her, but suspicions weren't enough. Nancy needed evidence.

Nancy examined Marianne's dresser top, careful not to move anything out of place. The items were typical: shampoo, conditioner, deodorant. There was a small framed photograph of Marianne in full police dress that Nancy hadn't noticed before.

Nancy glanced over at the closed door, hoping that Marianne wouldn't suddenly decide to return to the room. Knowing that she had to take the risk, Nancy opened the girl's top drawer.

Thirty pairs of gleaming white athletic socks were neatly folded and arranged in rows. Nancy was about to close the drawer when her eye was caught by the bright gleam of brass amid the white.

What's this? she wondered. Very carefully she reached under the socks and pulled out a pair of white gloves with brass buttons at the cuffs. Nancy held up the gloves and examined them. She checked the photo of Marianne on the dresser. The gloves matched the ones Marianne was wearing as part of her full-dress uniform.

I guess she keeps them for sentimental reasons, Nancy thought, but hoped otherwise. She knew from past cases that gloves could be a criminal's most important tool—they prevented fingerprints from being left behind.

She examined the gloves more carefully, hoping to find some telltale sign that they had been worn recently.

On the index finger of the right glove, she saw a tiny gray smudge. "Dried mud or dirt," Nancy murmured. "Marianne's such a neat freak—why would she keep a pair of soiled gloves?"

This could be the clue Nancy needed. She carried the glove to her own dresser. Opening her drawer, she pulled out a sealed plastic bag filled with barrettes and a pair of tweezers. "It may not be standard forensics equipment, but it will have to do," she said out loud.

Using the tweezers, she carefully removed some of the grains of dirt—or whatever it was— and dropped them into a plastic bag. She put the bag in her drawer. Later she would ask

Agent Burr to have the forensics lab examine the substance. She knew the agent wouldn't be happy to hear she'd been snooping again, but this substance just might provide an important clue to the case.

Nancy returned the gloves to Marianne's drawer, hoping she had put them back in their exact position. She closed the door and glanced at the clock again. Six forty-five.

I'd better go get Judy, Nancy thought. She hoped Joe really could keep Judy's attention as they jogged on the trail so she could talk to Frank. Judy seemed to think Joe was cute, and she knew that Joe wouldn't mind spending time with the attractive agent.

Nancy was halfway down the hall when she saw Jeff Abelson descending the stairs. To her embarrassment, she felt her heart beat a little faster.

"Hi, Nancy," Jeff said with a smile. He glanced at her sweats. "I see you're headed for some more PT."

Nancy saw that Jeff was dressed in his sweats, too. He had rolled up a bright blue bandanna and wound it around his head as a headband.

"Judy and I are going jogging," Nancy said.

"Judy? Are you sure you don't mean Frank Hill? I hear you two are an item," Jeff teased.

Nancy groaned. She should have guessed that Marianne couldn't keep anything secret.

"I wonder where you got that information," she said with a sheepish smile.

"I have my sources," Jeff said. "But if I'm wrong, how about taking me along with you and Judy? You can never tell what danger might lurk in those woods."

Nancy would have loved to, but she forced herself to turn him down. "Maybe some other time."

"Suit yourself," Jeff said easily. But Nancy thought she glimpsed a hurt expression on his face.

Nancy watched him go before knocking on Judy's door and entering. She was surprised to see that Judy was wearing jeans and a polo shirt. "Aren't we going jogging?" Nancy asked.

"Why don't you go on ahead, Nancy? I just realized how much studying I have to catch up on. Don't worry," she added wryly, "I'll make sure I don't stand next to the window."

Nancy hesitated. "Are you sure? I don't mind staying in."

"Sure I'm sure. No one will even know I'm here. Besides, I'm sure you could use a break from baby-sitting me," Judy assured her.

Nancy hated the idea of missing a chance to talk to Frank and Joe—especially since she didn't know whether Frank had recovered from his accident. She made up her mind to take Judy up on her offer. "I'll check on you as soon as I get in," she said.

The sun was low in the sky as Nancy headed for the jogging path through the woods. The twilight air was muggy, and Nancy had to swat away a few mosquitoes. She was glad to see Frank and Joe waiting for her at the head of the dirt trail.

"I was worried when I didn't see you two at dinner," Nancy said, taking in Frank's bandaged hands. "Are you all right?"

"I'm fine. These are just minor burns," he assured her. "It looks as though I won't be shooting a gun for a couple of days, though. We went back out to the firing range after the nurse checked me out. We wanted to see how someone could have sabotaged my shotgun."

"And?"

"That place is as secure as a bank vault, Nancy. The only way into the weapons cabinet is with a key."

"That means Banka had to do it," Joe said, "just as I thought."

"Or maybe," Nancy pointed out, "it was whoever's been shooting at Judy. Anyone who could steal ammunition could tamper with your gun."

"I just hope it doesn't mean we've blown our cover," Frank said slowly.

"Hey, where *is* Judy?" Joe demanded. "Don't tell me I've been stood up on our first jog together."

"She's in her room, studying," Nancy told him. "I think she really wanted to be alone. I didn't tell her she was missing out on you, though, Joe."

"I can't stand it," Joe grumbled. "First Erin starts fawning over Frank. Then Judy dumps me for schoolbooks. Come on, let's get this jog over with. If we're lucky, we can outrun these bugs."

Nancy laughed. The dirt crunched underneath their feet as the trio began running down the winding dirt path. The route they chose trailed along the Potomac River, although Nancy couldn't see much water through the dense trees. Even the sky was blocked by a canopy of leaves.

"Actually, there's a good reason why we missed dinner tonight," Frank said as they jogged. "Joe and I were looking at a package that a Network agent left us."

"Really? How does that work?" Nancy asked.

"The Network has agents in all arms of government. Apparently they even have one here at the academy," Frank said, "though for our own safety, we don't know who it is."

"Sounds spooky," Nancy commented.

"Anyway, while I was in the infirmary, Joe called the Gray Man," Frank continued. "He asked if the Network could find out whether Erin Seward filled out an application for a temporary parking pass."

Nancy remembered that the Gray Man was the code name for the Hardys' contact at the Network. He was the one who had gotten Frank and Joe involved with the organization.

"Yeah, it was amazing," Joe joined in. "When we got back from the infirmary, there was a folder on Frank's bed. In it was all the license plate information we requested yesterday, plus a copy of Erin's application."

Nancy ducked as she almost ran into a protruding tree branch. Sweat covered her forehead. "Did the pass tell you anything?" Nancy asked, turning her attention back to the Hardys.

"Not really," Frank said as they rounded a corner on the path. "Erin's application was for a brother, Jerry Seward. But there's no car on our list registered under that name."

"That would make sense," Nancy said, recalling Erin's file. "Erin is an only child, remember?"

Frank stopped dead in his tracks. "Of course!" he said, panting.

Joe stopped, too, gasping for breath. "That leaves us back where we started, then. We know Erin met someone last night, but we don't know who."

"I don't know about that," Nancy said. She bent over with her hands on her knees, trying to catch her breath. "It's not unusual for people using aliases to keep their own first names. Look at us."

"I see your point," Frank said. "All we have to do is check the list for anyone named Jerry or Gerald or Jerome. That should narrow it down."

Joe slapped Nancy on the back. "As usual, you're the best, Nancy Drew."

"Thanks, Joe," Nancy replied. Together, the trio started to jog again. It was starting to get dark, and Nancy was having trouble seeing the path in front of her. She wondered how Judy was doing back at the dorm.

"Listen," she said at last, "maybe we should turn—"

Nancy stopped as the woods echoed with a loud reverberation. She knew that sound, and it made her want to scream.

It was a gunshot.

Chapter

Ten

"Dive!" JOE HARDY SHOUTED, shoving Nancy to the ground and rolling with her off the jogging path.

"What are you doing?" Nancy shrieked, pulling away from him and sitting up in the underbrush. "That wasn't aimed at us. It was too far away."

"It sounded like it was closer to the river, and up a bit farther," Frank said from behind them. Nancy turned to see that Frank, too, had automatically rolled into the brush beside the path. As the three of them stood up, Nancy decided Frank must be right.

"I'll bet there's a path closer to the water," Nancy said, her heart racing. "Let's go!"

Nancy took off up the trail as fast as she could, Frank and Joe keeping pace. The loud retort of the gunshot still echoed in her ears. Someone could be in danger!

She nearly stumbled over a thick root that had grown onto the path but caught her balance at the last instant. The sun was sinking lower in the sky, and Nancy could barely see two feet in front of her. She tried to remain calm as the trees appeared to grow more menacing with each step. The sky above them had now turned a deep shade of crimson—blood red, Nancy thought, with a shudder.

"It looks like the path divides up ahead," she heard Frank call out.

Sure enough, the trail forked to the right a few yards ahead. Nancy paused for only a second to look down the arm of the trail.

"It seems to lead into a ravine," she said as she followed the new path.

The path led downhill, and it was steep. Nancy had to struggle more than once to maintain her footing.

She ran along the trail for about a hundred yards, straining to see if she could make out anything up ahead.

"Maybe we went the wrong way," she heard Joe say behind her.

"I'm sure the shot came from around here," Frank answered him.

Nancy peered off the side of the path and saw that the land did drop into a narrow ravine about ten feet into the woods, in the direction of the river. As she peered down into the ravine, Nancy froze.

"Frank! Joe!" she shouted, her heart pounding with apprehension. She walked to the edge of the path and peered closer. Yes, she was right. A body lay sprawled at the bottom of the ravine.

"What's wrong, Nancy?" Frank asked. He stepped up behind her, and Nancy pushed a branch aside, trying to make out the figure in the dim light.

"It's a woman," Nancy said. "She's lying face-down." The woman was wearing an academy sweat suit, and her shoulder-length blond hair was pulled back in a ponytail.

"Oh, no," Nancy said softly. She could barely get the words out. "That looks like Judy!"

Joe Hardy ignored the strain in his calves as he ran back up the path to get help. The trees beside him passed in a blur as he whizzed by. His mind was racing, too, as he tried to plot his best course of action. The infirmary was far across the campus. There would be a doctor on call and even an ambulance, but Joe was afraid that if the woman was still alive, he wouldn't make it there in time to save her.

If he followed the path that he, Frank, and Nancy had just taken, he would emerge out of the woods just a few hundred yards from the gym. There was a campus phone just outside the gym, he remembered. He could call the infirmary from there.

The woods began to thin out, and Joe could see the gym in the distance. He willed his legs to move even faster.

"Watch out!" someone yelled as Joe nearly tripped over him. Joe realized it was Jeff Abelson, doing warm-up stretches on the playing field between the woods and the gym. Jeff looked hot and sweaty, and Joe guessed that he had been out running, too.

"Sorry, Jeff. This is an emergency," Joe said, and continued running toward the gym.

Jeff stood up and began to follow him. "What happened?"

"Someone's been shot," Joe called back to him. "Didn't you hear anything?" It had seemed to Joe that the gunshot was loud enough to rouse the entire campus. If Jeff had been jogging in the woods, he should have heard it, Joe thought.

"No, I didn't," Jeff said. "Who was shot?"

Joe didn't answer. He had reached the campus phone and, grateful to see a special sticker with emergency numbers on the phone's base, was already dialing the infirmary number. He saw Jeff turn and run off toward the dorm.

Seconds later the phone was answered. "This is Agent Joe Hill. Someone's been shot in the woods. You've got to send a doctor," Joe said quickly. He tried to catch his breath.

"Where are you now?" a woman's voice asked.

"Outside the gym. The shot came from the jogging trail by the ravine. If you send someone here, I can show you where it happened. There's a body down there." Joe knew he was barely making sense.

"Someone will be right there," the woman said, and Joe hung up the phone.

He looked anxiously in the direction of the infirmary. "Please hurry," he said, half out loud. He leaned against a nearby tree. What if that really was Judy down at the bottom of the ravine? Joe remembered that the figure hadn't been moving. The thought that someone might have been shot and killed left a sick feeling in the pit of his stomach.

Just then Joe saw two figures emerge from the back doors of the gym. Joe thought he recognized Marianne Risi and Mike Banka. Joe flattened his back against the tree he was resting on. What are those two doing together? he wondered.

"You'll do it or I'll see that you're kicked out of the academy." Banka's words floated over the thick summer air to Joe. Joe strained to hear more, but was interrupted by the arrival of a small white vehicle that looked like a golf cart with a red light flashing on top.

A tall man in medical whites jumped out of the car. "Agent Hill? I'm Dr. Mendez," the man said. "Hop in."

Joe jumped into the cart. As they sped down

the path, he prayed that he and Dr. Mendez could reach the victim in time.

Nancy's heart beat wildly as she half ran, half stumbled down the ravine. She could hear Frank behind her.

"We're almost there, Nancy," Frank said. "I'm sure everything's okay."

"She's not moving, Frank!" Nancy cried. She couldn't panic. She decided now that the victim had to be Judy and she had to help her.

Why had Judy changed her mind and decided to go jogging? Nancy wondered. A chilling thought occurred to her. Maybe Judy had become scared or nervous alone in the dorm. She could have decided to try to find Nancy. I never should have left her alone, Nancy scolded herself. I was supposed to be her bodyguard, and I've failed. How could I have been so careless?

Frank passed Nancy, and she watched as he reached down and put a gentle hand on the girl's back.

"She's not breathing, Nancy," Frank said in a strained voice. Nancy watched in horror as Frank gently rolled the body over.

Frank was shocked as Nancy ran to his side.

Cradled in his arms was the lifeless body of Erin Seward.

Chapter

Eleven

"Move back," Frank said, bending over Erin's body. "I'll try CPR until someone gets here."

Nancy stood back, staring as Frank tried over and over to breathe life into the motionless girl.

"She's dead, isn't she, Frank?" Nancy managed to say as Frank pulled back for more air.

He hesitated, then stared stonily at the body. He hung his head miserably.

"Yes," Frank said softly. He laid Erin's head back onto the ground and stood up.

Nancy could make out a dark stain on the front of Erin's sweatshirt, and she knew that that was where the bullet had entered. "I still can't believe it," she said, tears welling up in her eyes. "Just a few hours ago she was sitting at our lunch table, telling us money wasn't everyth—"

Nancy couldn't go on—she knew she'd start crying if did. She stared without seeing into the dark woods that surrounded them. Was the killer still lurking there, watching them, listening to them?

"I'm going to search the area. Whoever shot Erin may still be here," Frank said.

"No, Frank, don't!" Nancy called as he started up the slope. "If the killer is still here, he or she has a gun, and you don't. You'll be an easy target. Joe should be here any minute with help."

"You're right, Nancy, as usual," Frank said, anguish and frustration visible on his face. "This is all so horrible. I wish there were something I could do."

"The most we can do for Erin now is find out who killed her—and make sure that person doesn't kill again," Nancy said passionately.

"You're right," Frank agreed. He shook his head. "What if that *was* the recruiter she met with the other night?" he said in a low voice. "Maybe Erin got cold feet and threatened to talk. She could have been shot to keep her quiet."

Nancy frowned. "Maybe, but I doubt it. As far as you know, has there ever been a murder connected with the Autowatch scam?"

"I don't think so," Frank admitted.

"That's what I figured. On the other hand, there *has* been a shooting at this academy recently, and the target was Judy Noll. That's why I convinced myself that was Judy lying there."

"So you think the shootings are related somehow," Frank suggested.

"It makes sense," Nancy said. "To tell you the truth, after I read in her file how much she'd wanted to go to law school but hadn't been able to pay for it, Erin became one of my main suspects in Judy's shooting. Now I wonder—"

Nancy glanced at Erin's body, then back at Frank. "Remember how certain I was that it was Judy down here? Erin and Judy are the same height and build, and they both wear their blond hair the same way. Judy usually runs at this time of day, and usually takes this trail. I'll bet the killer was waiting for Judy and shot Erin by mistake."

Frank let out a low whistle. "All the pieces seem to fit."

It made sense, Nancy knew. She shuddered. If it was true, then Erin's death was even more tragic.

Nancy's speculation was interrupted by the sound of an engine and branches snapping on the path above them. A vehicle was coming. Frank and Nancy hurried up the slope to wave the vehicle down. A small emergency cart pulled up, and a short, stocky man in medical whites jumped out from behind the steering wheel.

"She's down here, Doctor," Nancy called up to the man in white. Without a word, he hurried down into the ravine as Nancy made her way up.

"Nancy!" Joe cried, grabbing her by the arms. "Is Judy okay?"

"It isn't Judy. It's Erin Seward. She's been shot, Joe. She's dead," Nancy said.

"Oh, no—" Joe stopped abruptly, shaken, but quickly regaining his composure. "That's Dr. Mendez," he said, pointing toward the doctor. "We radioed security on the way over. An ambulance is on the way, but I don't think they'll make it down the path." Almost as proof of Joe's words, Nancy heard the wail of an ambulance approaching.

Nancy stared in the direction of the sound, and saw a large figure running down the path toward them. Mike Banka was approaching.

"What's going on, Agent Hill?" Banka demanded, red-faced and harried. "I was standing outside the gym when I saw the doctor's cart pull up, and then I saw you run toward it and jump in. What's happened?"

"Erin Seward's been shot," Joe said. "Didn't you hear the gunshot a few minutes ago?"

Banka shook his head. "I must have been inside the gym when it happened," he replied.

Joe's eyes widened in mock surprise. "You were in the gym, Agent Banka? What for?"

Nancy was surprised at Joe's asking Banka that question.

"I was in conference with one of the trainees," Banka said. "We met there, but I don't see what that has to do with anything," he added sharply.

Before Joe could reply, Nancy spotted the

beams of six flashlights bobbing through the woods. Agent Burr and five uniformed security guards ran up to them. Three of the guards broke off and began to explore the woods in their immediate area.

Burr rushed past Nancy and peered down into the ravine, shining his light on the doctor. "What's the word, Mendez?" he called down.

"Gunshot wound to the upper chest," Mendez replied. "It looks like the impact of the shot threw the victim off the trail. Then she probably rolled down the ravine. She appears to have been dead less than an hour."

Burr turned to Nancy. "All right, Agent Douglas, why don't you tell me what happened."

Nancy saw that Banka was observing her with keen interest. "I was jogging on the main path with Agents Frank and Joe Hill, sir," she said, adopting the respectful, serious tone she knew a trainee should use with a special agent. "Approximately a hundred yards back, we heard a gunshot. We determined that it came from this direction, approached, and then spotted the body at the bottom of the ravine. Joe Hill went for help, and Frank and I climbed down to see if we could help the victim. She was dead when we reached her."

"Did you alter the scene in any way or move the body?" Burr asked.

Frank stepped in front of Burr. "I did, sir. When we reached the bottom of the ravine, the body was facedown. I checked to see if the victim was breathing, and then I turned the body over to administer CPR."

"I see," Burr said. He seemed deeply disturbed. He removed a radio from his belt and snapped, "Get a forensics team down here immediately." Then he turned back to Nancy. "Agent Douglas, I'd like to speak with you."

Nancy followed Burr down the path, several feet away from the others. "What do you make of all this, Nancy?" Burr asked quietly.

Nancy told him her theory about Erin having been shot by mistake and Judy being the intended victim.

Burr nodded. "It's certainly possible," he agreed. He motioned toward Frank and Joe. "What do you know about the Hill brothers?"

For a moment Nancy was tempted to reveal the Hardys' identity to Burr. She wanted the agent to know her friends could be trusted. But she knew it would jeopardize the Hardys' case if she told the truth.

"They seem to be okay, sir," Nancy said. "Judy's very friendly with them. They were with me at all times on the path, so neither of them could have been responsible for the gunshot we heard."

"Good," Burr said. "It's lucky that I was working late tonight. Dr. Mendez called the main office for security backup, and I happened to overhear the request." He glanced back at the scene of the shooting. "This is a most disturbing turn of events. I'll understand if you want to call it quits, Nancy. You don't have any obligation to the bureau to continue."

Nancy shook her head. She couldn't give up now, especially after what had happened to Erin. "I'd like to stay on, sir, if that's okay with you."

Agent Burr hesitated. Nancy knew he didn't want her to get involved in the details of the case. Now that Erin had been killed, even Agent Burr had to understand that Nancy would do everything she could to try to solve the case.

"I think you've come up with some invaluable leads so far," Burr said at last with a weary sigh. "This is how we'll proceed. Our forensics team will spend the night combing the surrounding area for evidence—bullets, fingerprints, anything. I'll give you an update on that in the morning. In the meantime I'd like to get complete statements from you and the Hills."

"Yes, sir," Nancy said, trying not to let him see her relief and excitement.

"We should probably talk to Agent Banka, too. What was he doing here?"

"He saw Joe and Dr. Mendez take off in the emergency vehicle and followed them here," Nancy explained.

"I see," Burr said thoughtfully. "By the way, Nancy, why did you leave Judy alone?"

Judy! In a flash, Nancy realized that if the killer had gotten wind of the fact that it was Erin who had been shot, Judy's life could still be in danger.

"She's back at the dorm," Nancy explained quickly. "I have to—"

"Get going!" Burr said, finishing her sentence and tossing her his flashlight. Obviously he had made the same connection she had.

Nancy ran as fast as her legs could carry her. The path ahead seemed endless, but finally Nancy did see the lights of the main campus ahead.

She reached the dorm and took the steps two at a time to the second floor. After she pushed through the door to the hallway, she ran headfirst into Jeff Abelson.

"Whoops!" Nancy cried. Then she added, "What are you doing here?"

Still dressed in his sweats, Jeff seemed to be in as much of a hurry as she was. "Uh, nothing much," he said, shifting from one foot to the other. "Just, uh—looking for you!"

Nancy started to smile. Then she stopped. "But you knew I'd gone jogging," she said. "Why would you look for me here?"

"I thought you were back!" Jeff sounded almost desperate to get away. "See you later!" he added, sweeping past her without another word.

There's something strange going on here, Nancy told herself. Arriving at Judy's door, she pounded loudly. There was no answer.

"Judy!" Nancy called, pushing the door open. The room was empty.

"Don't panic," Nancy told herself. "She's

probably perfectly safe." Nancy spotted the clothes Judy had been wearing earlier draped over a chair.

"The shower!" Nancy said, running down the hall toward the shower room. As she neared the door, she could hear water running inside.

Thank goodness, Nancy thought, stepping inside, but her relief quickly turned to horror.

From out of the shower stall puffed large clouds of steam, and off the frosted glass door, moisture dripped on to the tiles. But instead of being clear, this water was brightly colored.

Nancy stared, aghast, at a river of liquid the color of blood running down the glass door and across the floor.

Chapter
Twelve

FOR AN INSTANT, Nancy was rooted to her spot. Then she raced to the shower door and flung it open wide.

"Hey!" Judy shouted, and reached out to close the door again.

"Judy! I'm glad you're okay," Nancy cried. "I'm sorry I scared you. It's just that the red stuff all over the door—"

"Oh, you didn't think—" Judy turned off the water and stepped out of the stall, wrapped in a towel. She touched some of the liquid on the door and held out her hand. "It's herbal shampoo. The bottle slipped out of my hands, and it splattered all over."

101

"I'm just glad you're all right," Nancy said.

"I told you it would be okay to leave me alone for a little while." Judy slipped into a white terry-cloth bathrobe.

A loud knock on the shower room door startled Nancy.

"Security! Is everything okay in there?" a male voice called.

"Of course it is!" Judy shouted. Then she turned to Nancy. "What's going on?" she asked.

Agent Burr must have radioed for a guard to check on Judy, Nancy realized. Suddenly the events of the past hour came flooding back. She dreaded having to tell Judy about Erin's terrible death.

"Let's go to your room, Judy. We need to have a talk," Nancy said.

Judy sobbed quietly as Nancy finished her story.

"I'm so sorry, Judy." Nancy sat on the bed next to Judy and put her arm around the woman. "I keep wishing there was something I could have done."

Judy brushed a tear from her cheek. "I feel silly, crying like this. I mean, I only knew Erin for a short time. But why would anyone want to harm her?"

Nancy hesitated. Judy deserved to hear her theory about Erin's shooting being a case of mistaken identity—Judy's safety could depend on it.

"I have a theory," Nancy began hesitantly, "and Agent Burr seems to agree."

Judy's eyes grew wide. "Wait a second, Nancy, I'm one step ahead of you. Do you think whoever is trying to kill me killed Erin by mistake?"

"That's exactly what we were thinking," Nancy said. "That's why I burst into the shower. I was afraid the killer might have realized his mistake and tried again to do the job right."

Judy began pacing the floor. "This is almost too much to handle. Erin's dead, and it's all because of me."

"Don't think like that, Judy. What happened wasn't your fault. There's a dangerous person out there." Nancy stood up. "Agent Burr needs to get a statement from me now, and I'd like you to come with me. I don't want to leave you alone again."

"You don't have to ask twice," Judy said, flashing a weak smile. "Just give me a minute to towel-dry my hair and get dressed."

Judy walked over to her closet and opened the door.

"Nancy, look at this!" she said, stepping back from the closet. "Someone's been in here!"

Nancy could see that most of Judy's clothes had been pulled off their hangers, and Judy's notebooks and textbooks were strewn on the closet floor.

"Let's check the rest of the room," Nancy said. She ran to Judy's dresser, which looked as if it had been similarly ransacked. Socks were sticking out of the drawers, and Judy's makeup and toiletries were scattered carelessly on the dresser's surface.

"We were so wrapped up in talking about Erin that we didn't even notice," Nancy remarked.

"Who could have done this?" Judy asked. "If the killer did come back after me, why didn't he just kill me? Why would he ransack my room?" Nancy could see that she was clearly frightened —perhaps even more frightened, somehow, than when she'd learned about Erin.

"I'm not sure," Nancy said. "Did you leave the room before you took your shower?"

Judy shook her head. "No. And I was only in the shower for five minutes before you came in. Whoever did this was just here."

Nancy remembered something. "Wait a minute. On my way up here I saw Jeff Abelson rushing out of this hallway. His room is on the fourth floor. He said he'd been looking for me— but then, when he found me, he ran away without talking. I wonder if anyone else saw him down here," she mused.

"You think *Jeff* did this? Why?" Judy sat back on the edge of her bed.

"Maybe you can tell me," Nancy said, her voice firm. "I'm going to check to make sure nothing dangerous was left here. Meanwhile, maybe you can tell me what Jeff might have been looking for. You told me that Jeff acts cool toward you because you wouldn't go out with him, but I never really bought that excuse."

"Well, I'm not sure myself," Judy said nervously as Nancy began systematically searching the room. "I mean, he did have the nerve to ask me out on the first day of training. Of course I said no. He's been nasty to me ever since."

Nancy straightened up from peeking under the bed. "I don't want to push this, Judy," she said impatiently, "but did you do or say anything else that might have made Jeff angry?"

"Angry enough to kill me?" Judy said with a bitter laugh. "I don't think so, but you never know."

"I don't see any bombs or explosives, at least. Let's not touch anything else. We might be able to lift some prints, and that could prove whether the intruder was Jeff or not. If it was, we'll have to figure out his motives."

"Good idea," Judy said. "Let's go see Agent Burr. I'm anxious to see what he thinks of all this."

Nancy's eyes followed Agent Burr as he paced back and forth across the short width of his office. His suit was perfectly creased, and his tie was tightly knotted, but Nancy could see the weariness in his eyes.

Judy, who sat in the chair beside Nancy's, had just told Agent Burr about her room being ransacked. Nancy realized that Burr barely registered what was said because he was so upset over the death.

"I got a call from the forensics team before you

came in," Burr was saying. "They can't tell much at this point, but they did retrieve the bullet. It was an academy-issue bullet from a .357 Magnum—the same kind of bullet that was used in your attempted shooting, Judy."

Judy nodded. "Nancy explained to me that Erin's death might have been a—well, a mistake. I suppose this supports that theory."

"Yes, it does," Burr replied.

"Were they able to determine anything else?" Nancy asked.

"It appears that Erin was shot from close range—no more than fifteen or twenty feet. Your hunch that the killer was waiting along the trail is probably right. I've assigned some special agents to the case. They're checking along the path for trace evidence right now," Burr said.

"What about the gun that was used? Is there any way to tie it to the gun that was used in the attack on Judy?" Nancy asked.

"That's a good question. All we know for sure is that both times, a .357 Magnum was used," Burr said. "As you know, that's one of the weapons the NATS use in firearms training. I have a man out at the firing range checking out all the Magnums there in the hope of finding a match."

"But that just brings us back to square one," Nancy said. "You and Agent Banka are the only ones with keys to the gun vault. Even if you do find a match, you still don't know who could have gotten access to those weapons inside, or how they could have done it."

"Actually, we have made some headway on that tonight," Burr said. He stopped pacing and leaned against his desk. "Agent Banka told me this afternoon that he'd discovered that someone had been tampering with his keys. He found the residue of what appears to be clay on one of the keys—the key to the gun vault."

"Clay? What does that have to do with anything?" Judy asked.

"Clay is often used to make an impression of a key," Nancy said excitedly.

"That's correct, Nancy," Burr said. "If someone made an impression of the key, they could make a copy of it and have easy access to the vault whenever Agent Banka wasn't there."

For the first time that night, Nancy's spirits brightened. "Could I see your key?" she asked. "In case I see the copy, it would be good to know what it looks like."

"It's rather ordinary, I'm afraid," Agent Burr said, taking out his key ring and showing Nancy the small brass key.

Nancy had to agree. She handed the key back and asked, "What's our next step?"

"Well, first I'd say we all need some sleep," the agent said. "Tomorrow morning the six agents I've assigned to this case will begin interrogating all the trainees and instructors who were on campus tonight to determine their whereabouts when Erin was shot. I'll also send someone first thing in the morning to dust Judy's room for prints. If we're lucky, we might just find something."

"I hope so. We need all the help we can get at this point," Nancy said.

Burr stood up. "I'll have a security guard escort you back to your dorm." He paused. "Judy, I've made this offer before, but I'd like to make it again. If you decide to drop out of the program, we'll be starting another class in five weeks that you can join."

Nancy watched Judy carefully. The woman's shoulders straightened, and a determined gleam shone in her eyes. "I've never been a quitter, Agent Burr. I'm not going to start now."

Burr dropped his gaze, clearly disappointed. "I understand, Agent Noll. But I'm afraid you may not have a choice. As we've witnessed today, your presence here poses a danger to the other trainees. The bureau may decide that it's better to remove you from the program."

Judy stiffened. "I'm sure my father would have something to say about that, sir. If you'll excuse us, it's been a long day. Let's go, Nancy," she said, and walked brusquely from the room.

Burr was surprised. Judy was flaunting her father's power openly.

Nancy wondered whether Burr knew how often Judy had angered the other trainees by referring to her father's wealth and influence. In any case, she decided, now was not the time to discuss it.

"Good night, Agent Burr," Nancy said.

"Good night, Agent Douglas," Burr said. "Be careful."

Judy was silent all the way back to her room. She simply lay down on her bed and closed her eyes when they got there.

"Good night, Judy," Nancy whispered after she had examined the room. She tiptoed out, quietly shutting the door behind her, wishing they had locks.

Nancy's own room was dark and quiet. Turning on the light, she saw that Marianne wasn't in yet. Nancy stretched her tired limbs. The run through the woods had taken its toll.

"A long, hot shower should do the trick," Nancy said out loud. As she changed into her bathrobe, she went over what Agent Burr had said. Finding clay on Banka's key was a stroke of luck, Nancy knew.

"Oh, wow. That's it!" Nancy cried, and pulled open her dresser drawer. She removed the plastic bag that she had collected the dirt in from Marianne's glove.

Holding the bag up to the light, Nancy carefully examined the sample. Just as she thought, it wasn't brown like dirt.

The material appeared gray and moist. That's because it's not dirt, Nancy realized—it's clay!

Chapter

Thirteen

"P LANNING ON MEETING your boyfriend again tonight?" Marianne asked.

Nancy jumped. She was so absorbed in what she was doing that she hadn't heard the door open. Fortunately, her back was to Marianne, so she could quickly slip the bag into her bathrobe pocket.

"If you mean Frank Hill, the answer is no," Nancy said, turning to face her roommate. "And besides, I didn't say he was my boyfriend. We just went for a walk, that's all."

"I didn't get this far in life by believing everything I'm told," Marianne said. "Hey, did you hear about Erin Seward?"

Nancy thought Marianne sounded more excited than concerned. "Yes, I did. How did you hear about it?" Nancy asked.

"I just came from the library. The word's out. It sounds like there's a psycho on the loose. I hear we're all going to be called in for questioning tomorrow morning."

"Yes, I know," Nancy said. Her mind was racing. If the clay on Marianne's glove matched the clay on Banka's key, then Marianne could very well be the killer. Nancy watched as her roommate nonchalantly laid out her clothes for the next day. Could a killer be so casual?

"I'm not worried. I have a perfect alibi," Marianne said confidently. "I was working out in the gym. Plenty of people saw me there. What about you, Douglas? I bet you were with Frank."

"As a matter of fact, I've already been questioned," Nancy said. She knew there was no sense in hiding the truth. "I discovered the body."

Marianne's eyes lit up. "Wow! That's going to look great on your record, Douglas."

Nancy thought she had seen Marianne at her worst before, but the young woman's insensitivity to Erin's death amazed her.

Nancy walked out and down the hall to the shower. Tomorrow I'll get my sample to Agent Burr, Nancy said to herself. Then maybe we'll finally find out the truth about Marianne Risi.

"Sleep late this morning, Nancy?" Joe Hardy asked as Nancy sat next to him at breakfast.

Frank and Judy were there also. Nancy had called the Hardys the night before and asked them to take Judy to breakfast and stay with her until she could join them.

"No, Joe. I had to see Agent Burr," Nancy replied, setting down her tray. Her blueberry muffin and glass of orange juice smelled wonderful. She was glad she hadn't missed breakfast altogether.

"The cafeteria seems awfully quiet this morning," Nancy remarked.

"Word has it that some of the NATS have been questioned already," Frank agreed.

Judy was staring into her bowl of uneaten cereal. "It was so quiet in my room this morning without Erin. I even missed arguing with her. It's just so unfair. Erin didn't deserve to die."

Joe put a protective arm around Judy's shoulders. "I'm sure Agent Burr will get to the bottom of this."

Nancy caught Jeff Abelson walking into the cafeteria and decided to try again to find out what Jeff was doing on the second floor the day before. "If you guys will excuse me, I'll be right back."

Nancy intercepted Jeff on his way to the food line. The young man flashed her a bright smile. Nancy noticed how good the green button-down shirt looked on him.

"I hear you were in the spotlight again last night," he said to her.

"What do you mean?" Nancy asked warily.

"Well, finding Erin's body and all," Jeff said. "I'm sorry, I didn't mean to make light of it. It must have been awful for you." He shook his head. "I have to say, though, you have an incredible nose for danger."

"Actually, I wanted to ask you about last night," Nancy said carefully. "Remember when I bumped into you in the dorm? You said you were looking for me, but when you found me, you were in a big hurry to get away."

Jeff seemed surprised by the question. "I got shy, I guess," he said. He added slyly, "Believe it or not, even I get tongue-tied sometimes."

Nancy felt herself blush, but this time Jeff's flattery failed to distract her. "Something weird happened right after you left," she said. "Judy and I discovered that somebody had ransacked her room. You didn't see anybody in the hallway, did you?"

"I don't think so," Jeff said. "But then, I was kind of in a hurry."

Nancy didn't believe a word of what he had said. "Well, it doesn't matter. They're dusting Judy's room for prints right now. We should have a better idea of who was in the room very soon," she told him.

Jeff grabbed Nancy's right arm. "Listen, Nancy, I know you and Judy are friends," he said. His voice was low and shaky, and Nancy thought he seemed much less confident. "But Judy isn't everything she seems to be. Just remember that, okay?"

"What do you mean—" Nancy began.

"We're going to be late for PT, Nancy," Frank cut in, appearing at her side just then. He quickly pried Jeff's hand from Nancy's arm. "You don't have a problem with that, do you, Abelson?"

"Sorry, Hill, I didn't mean to move in on your territory," Jeff said smoothly. He stepped away, his old self again. "See you two later."

"Frank, what did you do that for? I was about to make a breakthrough!" Nancy exclaimed as she watched Jeff disappear down the cafeteria line.

"I thought he was hassling you, Nancy. I was just trying to help," Frank said.

"Just try to remember that I'm not helpless, okay?" Nancy checked back at their table. "Where are Joe and Judy?"

"Joe offered to walk Judy over to PT. I think my little brother's developing a crush," Frank said.

Nancy smiled. "Well, I happen to know that Judy thinks Joe is cute—but young," she said.

"I'm sure Joe will get over it," Frank said. "Anyway, I thought this would give us a chance to talk."

"We need to. You won't believe some of the things I've found out," Nancy said. As they walked across the campus, she told Frank about running into Jeff in the hallway, the discovery in

114

Judy's room, and finally about the possible connection between Marianne and the key to the gun vault—all clues that might help her discover who had been threatening Judy.

"You've certainly been busy. Have you had time to put the pieces together?" Frank asked.

"Not really. The things that happened last night lead in two different directions—either Jeff or Marianne could be involved. Maybe even both! There are still too many missing pieces to the puzzle," Nancy said.

Frank nodded. "How would you like to do some joint sleuthing, Nancy? To investigate Erin's death."

"Sure," Nancy said. "What do you have in mind?"

"I thought we could get Arnold Hoffman to go to the crime scene with us tonight. He's a forensics genius. We could ask him to let us use the experience as an exercise to test our new forensics skills."

"Good idea," Nancy agreed. "But Hoffman is an instructor. Have you considered him a suspect in your case at all?"

"Every instructor is a suspect, of course," Frank said. "But the Network has nothing on him. And Joe's been doing his best to fail forensics, but Hoffman hasn't taken the bait yet. He seems pretty trustworthy."

"Then let's go for it," Nancy said.

* * *

"Thanks for helping me put Erin's things together," Judy said to Nancy. They were both sitting cross-legged on the floor of Judy's room.

"No problem," Nancy said. "I didn't feel like eating lunch, anyway. I can't get my mind off this case." PT had seemed to drag on forever that morning, Nancy thought, and so had the class on interrogation methods. It was only Nancy's third day in the training program, yet she couldn't seem to concentrate on anything.

Nancy continued folding Erin's T-shirts and placing them into the black steamer trunk that Erin had brought with her to the academy. "Is Erin's aunt picking this stuff up today?" she asked Judy.

"As far as I know." Judy set down the pile of notebooks she was holding. "This is all so sad."

"I know," Nancy agreed. As she put another shirt into the trunk, a scrap of paper poking out of the trunk's lining caught her eye.

"What's this?" Nancy reached behind the loose lining. She pulled out a small bundle of newspaper articles that had been neatly clipped together.

"What are they?" Judy asked. She leaned over Nancy's shoulder.

"They're articles from the *Washington Observer*," Nancy said, leafing through them. "All written by somebody named Jerry Nieves, and they seem to be about the same story. 'Lawyers Accused in Farm Scandal,' 'Farm Fraud in Iowa.' I wonder why she had these," Nancy said.

Judy grabbed one of the articles from Nancy's hand. "Who knows why? Maybe she knew someone involved. I'm sure it's nothing important."

Nancy shook her head. "I don't know. Why would Erin have gone to the trouble of hiding them in the lining of her trunk? You're from Iowa, aren't you, Judy? Do you know anything about this farm scandal?"

"Not a thing," Judy said, handing the article back to Nancy. "I think I've heard of Jerry Nieves, though. He's one of those reporters who's always stirring up trouble. My dad says he's a notorious liar."

Suddenly Nancy had an idea. Her mind racing, she gathered the articles and stuffed them into her bag. "Judy, can you finish packing Erin's things? I'm sorry, but I've got to do something really important. I'll have Agent Burr send over a security guard to stand out in the hall. I'll be back in time to walk you to the firing range."

Without waiting for an answer, Nancy headed out the door. She had to find the Hardys immediately. If her hunch was right, she might have found a vital clue to help them solve their case. And if she solved the Hardys' case, she thought wistfully, maybe they would solve hers.

As she called for a guard from the phone in the lounge, Nancy glanced at her watch. It was 12:40. Frank and Joe should be changing into their firearms gear about now. She waited impatiently until the guard arrived, then took the stairs two at a time to the third floor.

"Frank! Joe! Are you in there?" Nancy called softly, rapping on their door. "I have to talk to you."

"Just a minute," Frank said. In a few seconds the door creaked open, and Nancy stepped inside. Frank was already in his loose trousers with his firing range earmuffs around his neck. Joe sat on the edge of his bed, lacing up his combat boots.

"Is everything okay?" Frank asked.

"Everything's fine. Listen, do you have that list of car owners that the Network gave you?"

"Sure," Frank said. "Just give me a minute." Frank bent down and reached under one of the beds, pulling out a large suitcase. He opened it and pulled a folder from a hidden compartment.

"These false bottoms come in handy," Frank said, handing Nancy the folder.

Joe rose from the bed and peered at the folder over Nancy's shoulder. "So what's the big secret?" he asked impatiently. "Do you think you know who met with Erin the other night?"

"I'll let you know in a second," Nancy said. She scanned the list carefully. There were hundreds of names, but luckily they were in alphabetical order.

"Nance, Neelan," Nancy muttered. In a few seconds she found what she was looking for.

"Bingo!" she cried.

"What is it, Nancy? What did you find?" Joe asked, his voice betraying his excitement.

Nancy put the folder down on the bed in front of them. "Gentlemen, I think I've found our mystery man—the guy Erin met with the other night. His name is Jerry Nieves."

Chapter

Fourteen

JERRY NIEVES? That name sounds familiar," Frank remarked.

"He's a reporter for the *Washington Observer*," Nancy said. She showed Frank and Joe the articles she had brought with her. "Judy and I found these in Erin's trunk. They're all written by Nieves. And his name appears on your list."

"It sure looks as if he's our man," Joe said thoughtfully. "But what could she have been giving him? And does this have anything to do with either of our cases?"

"I'm not sure," Nancy replied. "I'll have to read these articles carefully and then find out if Agent Burr has any information on him."

"But, Nancy," Frank said, "if you tell Burr we

watched Erin pass information to this Nieves guy, you could blow our cover. And how are you going to explain this list to him?"

"How do you know Agent Burr doesn't already know who you are?" Nancy asked. "He's pretty important in the FBI, you know."

"I don't think so," Joe remarked. "The Network sent us here to investigate the bureau. It wouldn't make sense for them to inform the bureau ahead of time."

Nancy sighed. "I guess you're right. This will be hard to explain without dragging you guys into it. But I can't keep this from him."

"I have a suggestion," Joe said. "Why don't you call Nieves? He could have a reasonable explanation for coming here. If he acts suspicious, we'll think of a way to tell Burr about him."

"Good idea," Nancy said. "I'll try to call him right now."

Frank checked his watch. "You're going to be late for firearms training. How are you going to explain that to Banka?"

"Could you tell him Burr needed me to do some more translations?" Frank nodded.

"One more favor—could you walk Judy to the range? I don't want to leave her alone after last night."

"You bet! We'll go get her now," Joe said, and started down the stairs.

"Watch out, Joe," Nancy heard Frank say as she waited for the hall to clear so she could use the pay phone near the stairs. "Audrey might get mad. I saw the way you were cozying up to her in PT this morning."

"Cozying up?" Joe retorted from the stairwell. "I just wanted to make sure she didn't flip me again! At least Judy doesn't humiliate me in public."

Nancy laughed. Cases involving the Hardys were never boring.

A few minutes later, the hall was quiet. Nancy took her credit card from her wallet and used it to dial Washington, D.C., information to get the number of the *Observer*.

"I'd like to speak to Jerry Nieves, please," Nancy said after her call went through.

"I'll connect you to the national news desk," a female voice said.

Nancy heard a few clicks, and then a male voice said, "National."

"My name is Nancy Douglas. I'm trying to contact Jerry Nieves," Nancy said.

"You and a million other people," the man said, laughing. "Jerry's been away researching a story for the last few days. Nobody's sure where he is."

Nancy's heart sank. "Do you know when he'll be back?" she asked.

"Try again on Sunday."

"Thanks." Nancy hung up the phone.

Sunday. It was Friday. There was nothing to do but wait.

* * *

Frank Hardy scanned the campus for any sign of Nancy and Judy. It was seven o'clock, and he, Joe, and Agent Hoffman were waiting outside the gym for the girls to arrive.

"Thanks for agreeing to go to the site with us, Agent Hoffman," Frank said. "I'm sure Agent Douglas and Agent Noll will be here any minute." Frank knew that Nancy had told Judy that the Hill brothers had come up with the brilliant idea of examining the site, and that it was a perfect opportunity for them to search for clues to the identity of Judy's attacker.

"It's my pleasure, Agent Hill," Hoffman replied. "And your brother Joe here can certainly use the experience. He doesn't seem to have a very good grasp of the science of forensics."

Joe grinned sheepishly. "Frank was always the brains of the family."

Frank smiled at his brother. He knew how hard it was for Joe to have to say such a thing, even if it was to protect their cover.

Hoffman was smiling at Joe, too, Frank noticed. The agent had on a lightweight gray suit and red tie—a popular choice of clothing for the instructors, Frank reflected. He was carrying what looked like a black doctor's bag. He tried to look businesslike, but with his graying hair and soft brown eyes, he resembled a kindly grandfather most.

"Don't worry, Joe," Hoffman said. "I'm sure we'll find a way to improve your performance in class. You have a great deal of potential."

Joe beamed at Hoffman's compliment. "Thanks, Agent Hoffman. I really am looking forward to studying the site of the shooting with you."

"You know, I'm curious about you two," Hoffman said after a moment of silence. "Do you mind if I ask you a few questions?"

Startled, Frank tried not to show it. "Not at all, sir. What kind of questions?"

"Well, I was wondering . . ." Hoffman hesitated. "We've never had a pair of brothers before," he began. "What made you decide to train together, and what was your experience before then?"

"It's in our file, sir," Joe said quickly. "We work in computers. We're programmers, both of us. We grew up in—San Jose."

"San Jose?" Hoffman cocked his head, intrigued. "I could have sworn you were from San Diego."

Frank saw Joe obviously searching his brain to remember what the Network background had said about them.

"We were born in San Diego," Frank spoke up in a clear voice. "But we grew up in San Jose. That's where most of the computer industry is, Agent Hoffman. Do you know a lot about computers?"

Fortunately, the conversation was cut short by the appearance of Judy and Nancy.

"Here come the girls," Frank said, greatly

relieved. "We should get going. We're starting to lose our light."

"Hi, guys," Nancy said when she and Judy reached the group. "Sorry we're late. Erin's aunt came to pick up her things."

"It isn't going to be easy going to the place where Erin was killed," Judy said.

Agent Hoffman put an arm around her. "It's never easy, Judy," he said sympathetically, "but it's part of being an agent."

Judy nodded. "I know. It sure is different from law school, though."

Frank fell in step beside Judy. If the killer tried anything tonight, he'd have to deal with Frank Hardy first.

The group was silent until they came to the fork in the path. "It's this way." Frank headed down the right fork.

"We're almost there," Frank said. A few yards up, the path was blocked off with white tape that read, Federal Crime Scene. Do Not Cross.

"Don't worry about that tape," Hoffman said. "I'm authorized to investigate the area." He stepped forward, adding, "To tell you the truth, I'm glad to make it down here. I've been too busy to take a look."

Frank lifted up the tape to let Nancy and Judy slip under. Hoffman and Joe followed.

Hoffman turned to Frank. "Where exactly did you find the body?"

Frank peered down into the ravine. "Down

there," he said, pointing. "You can see the path that Erin's body took by the crushed shrubbery going down the slope."

"Very observant, Agent Hill," Hoffman said. "Now, I've made copies of the preliminary forensics report. Would everyone like a copy?" He passed them out.

"What do you make of it, Agent Douglas?" Hoffman asked at last.

"Well, this report says it's believed that the shot was fired from about ten feet away," Nancy said. "So I guess it would be possible to determine almost exactly where the shot was fired from."

"Correct," Hoffman said. Frank watched as he positioned himself in the middle of the trail next to the spot where Erin had begun her descent down the slope.

"Let's say that I am the victim. From what I understand, the bullet entered here," he said, placing his hand just above his heart. "Now, I don't have any surveying equipment with me, but with this knowledge we can approximate the direction that the shot came from."

"I think I understand, sir," Frank said. He stood directly in front of Hoffman with his back to the instructor. "If I walk ten feet in this direction, we can figure out where the killer was hiding."

"As I said, it won't be one hundred percent accurate, but, yes, we should get an excellent idea," Hoffman said.

Frank carefully measured out ten paces. As he counted off the last step, he found himself face-to-face with a large oak tree.

"Someone could have hidden behind this tree," Frank said. From behind the tree he could clearly make out the instructor on the path. "If our guess is right, the killer would have had a clear shot from here."

"Very good, Agent Hill," Hoffman said. "Now let's head down the ravine and take a closer look at the area in which the body was discovered."

Frank hesitated. Seeing Hoffman on the trail had given him an idea.

"I'll be right down, sir," Frank said. "I'd like to check out this area a little longer, if that's okay."

"I'd like to look around up here, too," Nancy said.

Hoffman started down the ravine, with Joe right behind. But Frank saw Judy hesitate at the ravine's edge.

"I'll be okay," Frank heard Judy tell Joe, who had stopped to wait for her. "I just need to prepare myself, that's all."

Frank and Nancy waited until Hoffman, Joe, and Judy had climbed down before they spoke. "What's up, Frank?" Nancy asked.

"I think I have a way to test your theory about the killer mistaking Erin for Judy," Frank said. He walked behind the oak tree. "I'll stand here where the killer probably was. If you jog down the path, I'll be able to tell if I can see your face clearly."

Nancy checked the sky. "It's about the same time we heard the shot yesterday."

Frank ducked behind the tree as Nancy jogged back up the path. He crouched on one knee, waiting for his target to approach.

A moment later he heard Nancy's footsteps on the dry path. He ignored the dark shadows the trees were casting across the trail and fixed his eyes on the point where Erin had been shot.

Nancy came into view. Frank noticed that her hair was pulled back in the style Judy usually wore.

Crunch! Nancy's foot crushed a twig as she jogged closer.

From where he was crouched, Frank could clearly make out Nancy's face. There was no mistaking it.

This could mean only one thing, Frank realized. Judy hadn't been the killer's target after all!

Chapter

Fifteen

"**W**HAT DID YOU SEE?**" Nancy called as she slowed from a jog to a walk.

"I saw *you,* Nancy," Frank said. "There was no mistaking your face."

Nancy recognized the tone in Frank's voice. She heard it whenever he was on the verge of an important breakthrough.

"Do you mean that there was no way the killer could have mistaken Erin for Judy?" Nancy asked.

Frank shook his head. "Not unless the killer was blind as a bat, and we already know he was too good a shot for that. If Erin was the killer's target, that means she probably had nothing to do with the attacker who's been stalking Judy. But she could still have something to do with the recruiting ring."

"I'm not so sure, Frank," Nancy replied. "Maybe she had nothing to do with either case."

"Maybe." Frank moved closer to Nancy and lowered his voice. "Or maybe she was involved in both. Nancy, what if Judy had gotten mixed up with the recruiter somehow? Maybe that shooting last week was a warning, and Judy took it. Maybe the recruiter warned Erin, too, but Erin ignored the warning."

"So the recruiter killed Erin?" Nancy couldn't believe what Frank was suggesting. "Judy doesn't fit the Autowatch profile at all. Also, don't you think she would have said something about it?"

"And risk ruining her father's reputation? I don't think so," Frank replied.

"I guess it's possible that the two attacks are linked somehow," Nancy admitted. "But something tells me that the Autowatch scam isn't the answer."

Nancy and Frank's conversation was interrupted by Hoffman's voice. "Did you two find anything up here?" he asked as he climbed out of the ravine. Joe and Judy were right behind him.

"Not really," Nancy replied. They wanted to tell only Agent Burr about their discovery. "How about you?" Nancy asked.

Hoffman brushed some dirt off his hands and straightened his glasses. "Nothing. The forensics team did an excellent job examining the site."

"It's getting dark," Joe remarked, wiping the sweat from his forehead. "What do you say we head back?"

"You're always anxious to get out of class, aren't you, Joe?" Hoffman teased. "I have a flashlight in my bag here, and I'd like to have a look at that tree myself, if nobody minds," he said, pointing to the oak.

"That's a great idea," Nancy said.

The group followed Hoffman back to the tree. He put his black bag on the ground and took out a small flashlight and a magnifying glass.

"Let's take a look at the bark first," the instructor said. "Things often get caught on it: hair, clothing, even skin."

Nancy watched as Hoffman carefully pored over the surface of the tree. Only the chirp of crickets penetrated the silence of the woods as Hoffman worked.

In a few minutes Nancy saw a smile cross Hoffman's face. "Could someone please hand me the tweezers and a plastic bag?"

Hoffman carefully plucked something off the bark and emptied the tweezers into the bag. He illuminated the bag with the flashlight and held it up for Nancy and the others to see. Inside were a few frayed blue threads.

"This appears to be a shred of clothing," Hoffman said.

Joe was puzzled. "What can you tell from a little scrap of blue stuff?" he asked.

"If you paid more attention to my lectures, you

would know," Hoffman said. "Can anyone here help him?"

"I think I can," Judy volunteered. "The lab can analyze that to see what kind of cloth it is. They can even tell how old or new it is. Then you can compare it to clothing owned by people here at the academy until you get a match."

"That's correct, Agent Noll," Hoffman said, smiling broadly. "I'll report this find to Agent Burr, and we'll begin to take the steps you just mentioned. In the meantime I think we should head back."

At the mention of Agent Burr's name, Nancy's mind clicked. She had to talk to him about her and Frank's discovery. If she was lucky, he would still be in his office.

Nancy took Judy aside as the others started back up the path.

"Judy, I need to stop by Agent Burr's office for a little while," Nancy said. "Can you get Frank and Joe to walk you back to the dorm? I'll be back before lights out."

"Sure, Nancy," Judy said. "Do you think you have some answers?"

"I'm not sure," Nancy replied. "But I hope we'll have some soon."

Half an hour later Nancy had explained to Special Agent Burr that because of her experiment with Frank, she believed that Erin really was the killer's target. "What's your opinion of all this, then?" he asked uneasily.

"Well, at first I wasn't sure why someone would want to hurt both Erin and Judy. I couldn't imagine how they could be linked," Nancy said. "Then I remembered the obvious: They both had shoulder-length blondish hair. They were both kind of tall and slim. I thought that maybe, well—do you think there could be a simple physical pattern here?"

Burr stopped pacing. "You mean, someone's stalking the area looking for blond women? What for?"

"I don't know," Nancy replied. "But if a criminal is attacking only certain types of people, how do you go about trying to catch him?"

"We would use a decoy—an agent who looks like the previous victims," Burr said. He was eyeing Nancy uncomfortably.

"Exactly," she said calmly. She knew that physically she was similar to Erin and Judy. "I'd like to volunteer to be a decoy."

Burr stared at her, his face flushed. "Nancy, I couldn't allow that," he protested. "You're a civilian, not an agent."

"Yes, but I'm also a trainee here, and I could easily double for Judy or Erin," Nancy said. "I'm your only logical choice at this point."

"I don't care! It's preposterous, putting an eighteen-year-old girl in such a position. I'll find an experienced agent to do the job."

"But I am experienced, Agent Burr," Nancy insisted, leaning forward. "I've been involved in dangerous detective work for ages. Besides," she continued hesitantly, seeing that he wasn't willingly going to change his mind, "I'm already too involved in this case. If you pulled me out now, I'd probably be so upset, I'd have to go tell the papers about it."

Burr froze and glared at her. "Is that a threat?" he asked in a low voice.

"Not exactly, sir," Nancy replied cautiously. "It's a sign of how sure I am you'll give me the job. I'm ready to start right away."

Burr hesitated. He picked up a pencil and began tapping it on the edge of his desk. "It would have to be an extremely controlled situation. I couldn't place you in any more danger than you're already in," he said at last.

"Maybe we could get Frank and Joe Hill involved somehow," Nancy suggested. "It happens that I've known them for years. You were satisfied with their alibis when you interviewed them earlier, weren't you?"

"Certainly. Along with all the other trainees' alibis," Burr pointed out. "If the killer is one of our newcomers, he's certainly fooled me. Now," he added, "I suppose you already have a plan in mind."

Nancy smiled. She didn't relish the thought of acting as bait to be murdered. But someone had to stop whoever had killed Erin. "What if we set up a special event tomorrow?" Nancy suggested. Briefly she outlined her idea.

* * *

Nancy knew that Burr had successfully set her plan into motion as she walked toward the shower that morning. A group of NATS, many still in bathrobes, had gathered around a notice posted on the wall of the lounge. Audrey LaFehr was reading the notice out loud.

"Survival training! What will they think of next?" Audrey moaned.

"What's going on?" Nancy asked, joining the group.

"You mean you haven't heard, Douglas?" Marianne said. "We're all supposed to report to the outdoor obstacle course at eight o'clock this morning for an all-day survival program."

"It's not fair. I need the time to study," Audrey complained. It was Saturday, and Nancy knew Saturdays were usually left free for students to study.

"Speak for yourself," Marianne said, stretching out on the lounge floor. "This is going to be great. I say whoever makes the best time today buys pizza for the whole second floor."

Nancy was glad that word seemed to be getting around about the all-day survival course. Nancy and Agent Burr had decided that trainees would be sent out into the woods in groups of three. Nancy, Frank, and Joe would be the first group. Nancy would be an obvious target in the woods.

"Hey, Douglas, you'd better get moving," Marianne said. "We've got to be there in an hour."

* * *

One hour later Nancy stood at the edge of the woods in a sea of regulation gray sweats. Behind her, the first of a series of obstacles—a double row of tires through which the trainees would have to run—lay half-hidden in the underbrush a hundred yards away. All of the NATS in Nancy's class were present, as was Samantha Havlicek. She was clearly annoyed at having to oversee this last-minute exercise.

"Nervous, Nancy?"

Nancy jumped at the sound of Joe's voice behind her. Frank was next to him.

"Don't scare me like that, Joe! Of course I'm nervous," Nancy said. She glanced around to make sure no one was listening. "Do you know what's going on?"

"Burr briefed us this morning," Frank said. "He said we should keep an eye on you in the woods, and also on the other trainees to see if anyone's interested in where you go or what you do. He said he's going to have agents hidden all along the trail. You'll be covered from all sides, Nancy," Joe reassured her.

"I know," Nancy said. "I just hope it works."

Samantha Havlicek's whistle pierced the air. "All right, people. Listen up!"

Nancy walked over to stand beside Havlicek on the painted white line that marked the beginning of the course. The course began farther away from the river than the trail they had followed the night before. The trees were not quite so thick here.

When the crowd quieted down, Havlicek cleared her throat. "As an agent, you might find yourself alone in a dangerous situation. This exercise should prepare you for those situations," she began. "As you have already read, we've expanded the outdoor obstacle course. We'll be sending you out in groups of three. One individual in a group will leave every five minutes. Each group will leave every half hour. The course should take approximately two hours to complete. You will be scored on your ability to complete the obstacles and the time of completion. The first group, consisting of Agent Douglas, Agent Frank Hill, and Agent Joe Hill, will begin in exactly one minute. Please see me for group assignments for the rest of the day. You will be allowed to study while waiting for your turn."

The NATS began to crowd around Havlicek. Nancy stepped away from the group. If the killer was nearby, he or she would know that Nancy would soon be alone in the woods.

Audrey and Jeff walked up to Nancy and patted her on the back. "Good luck, Nancy," Audrey said. "That's awful—going first. I don't have to go until two o'clock."

"I don't have to go until noon," Jeff said. He seemed oddly uncomfortable, Nancy thought, as though he had something important to say.

"I wish I could trade places with you, Douglas," he said abruptly.

"That's okay," she said, managing a smile. "I'd rather get it over with."

"No, I mean it," he said, embarrassed as she stared at him. "I wish I could do it for you."

"That's very nice, Jeff," Nancy said. "I'll think of you while I'm running."

"Great," Jeff said. Unexpectedly, he gave her a quick hug.

Havlicek's whistle pierced the air again. "Douglas! Frank! Joe! Front and center, please!"

Nancy joined the Hardys at the starting point. Havlicek stood next to them, holding a stopwatch. "Joe, you go first, then Douglas, then Frank. Begin when the whistle blows. Got it?"

"Got it," Joe said. Still holding the watch, Havlicek blew the whistle, and Nancy watched Joe disappear into the woods ahead of her.

The next five minutes were a lifetime to Nancy. She had to wipe the sweat from her palms more than once before the whistle signaled her turn. She glanced over her shoulder, trying to keep track of Marianne, Judy, Jeff, and the others who wandered around the area.

The whistle sounded. Nancy took off like a shot. Some of the NATS let out a cheer behind her, but their cries grew dim as she headed deeper into the woods.

Soon Nancy came across the two rows of tires that stretched along the trail for twenty feet.

"One, two, one, two," Nancy counted, trying to keep her balance as she stepped into the center of each tire. By alternating her feet in perfect rhythm, she made it through the course easily.

Nancy ran farther into the woods. She tried to pace herself—if the plan didn't work, she still had a two-hour course to complete, and she wanted to make sure she finished it.

The tall trees flew by. Nancy couldn't shake the feeling that someone was watching her. Is there a special agent hiding behind one of these trees? Nancy wondered, or is it the killer lurking?

Nancy jogged for about twenty minutes. She came upon a few forks in the trail, but some of the branches were roped off by tape. The path seemed to be moving her closer and closer to the river. Soon she found herself on the edge of the ravine where Erin had been shot.

Two ropes had been stretched across the ravine, one higher than the other. The path was blocked on either side of her. To continue the course, she'd have to cross the ravine.

"Here goes nothing," Nancy muttered, taking a deep breath. She jumped up and grabbed hold of the lower rope. Hand over hand, she worked her way across the ravine. A quick glance down told her she was about fifty feet in the air.

"Come on, Nancy," she said, her arms straining under her own weight. "You're halfway there."

Nancy was reaching for another section of the rope when a loud explosion filled the air. In the same instant Nancy felt her heart drop to the pit of her stomach as the rope gave way. She reached out to grab something—anything—but all she got was a handful of air.

With a scream, Nancy felt herself tumbling backward—flying toward the ground below on a length of rope!

Chapter

Sixteen

FRANK'S HEART trip-hammered as the shot pierced the air. He watched Nancy dangling wildly on the end of her rope.

"Nancy!" he shouted, his pace quickening to a mad dash. The fact that the killer could easily squeeze off a shot at him barely registered in his brain.

As he reached the mouth of the ravine, Frank shouted, "Throw your weight! Swing toward me!"

For a long moment Nancy didn't seem to hear Frank. He worried that she might have gone into shock. Then, gradually, she started to swing back and forth on the rope, trying to arc far enough to land beside Frank on the opposite side of the ravine.

"Hurry, Nancy," Frank said, glancing around for any sign of the gunman. "You can do it."

Nancy swung farther with each effort. Soon she was swinging nearly as high as Frank's head. "Okay, Nancy," Frank yelled excitedly. "When I say three, jump!"

"One! Two!" The rope swung toward Frank, then away again.

"Three!" Frank held out his arms to catch her. He watched Nancy's hands let go of the rope. She fell in a smooth arc—down, down, down—

"Watch out!" Frank shouted, running forward. He nearly fell into the ravine before he caught himself. Nancy was not so lucky. Her leap from the rope had fallen short, and Frank watched in horror as she landed against the side of the ravine.

"Nancy!" he yelled, sliding down the slope to her still form.

His apprehension melted as Nancy smiled weakly at him. "I'm okay," she reassured him, taking the hand he offered to help her to her feet.

"Easy," Frank said. Nancy had received no visible wounds, but she was shaken. Her face was white.

"You'd better sit down, low, until help comes, Nancy," Frank advised. "You may be hurt. Besides, the gunman could still be out there."

Nancy shook her head. "Not with all of the agents combing the grounds. He or she would have to make a quick getaway. I don't think there's anything to worry about."

Just then they heard Joe calling Nancy's name. "We're down here!" Frank shouted. A moment later Joe's worried face peered down at them.

"Are you two okay?" Joe asked.

"We're fine," Nancy said. "Get help."

"It's already here," Joe replied.

Joe stepped aside to reveal a half dozen armed agents, wearing navy blue pants, caps, and vests. Agent Havlicek was with them. Frank guessed that she had taken a shortcut to the site after hearing the shot.

"Are you okay?" she demanded, staring at the rope that dangled over the ravine.

"Frank and I are fine, but we're not so sure about Nancy. She was on the rope when it was shot at and she fell," Frank told her.

"The medics are on their way. Did you see anything?" Havlicek asked. She was holding a small black radio.

"We didn't see anyone," Frank replied, the muscles in his face tense. "Wait a minute. You knew about this operation?"

"Agent Burr informed me first thing this morning," Havlicek replied grimly. "I understand it has something to do with Judy Noll's situation, and that's all I know."

She then turned her attention to the group of special agents beside her. "I want every inch of this area covered. The perpetrator has a long lead, so get moving."

When the others had dispersed, Nancy said to Frank and Joe, "Don't you think we should look around for clues while we're waiting? No one's checking here at the edge of the ravine."

Frank marveled at Nancy's steely nerves. No one ever would have guessed what she had just been through. "All right," he agreed. "Joe and I will search. You stay there until we know for sure you're all right," Frank said.

Frank and Joe climbed to the top of the ravine and began to comb the ground. "The gunshot sounded as if it was close by," Frank said. "From what we've learned in forensics class so far, I'd say it came from the northeast. I wouldn't go beyond a hundred feet looking for clues."

"Bingo," Joe called out a few moments later. "Come over here."

Frank followed Joe's voice to a tree several feet from the ravine. His brother pointed to a blue strand of fabric snagged on the bark.

"It looks like the same material we found near Erin's body," Frank said.

"I guess when we find the owner of this shirt or pants, we'll have our shooter," Joe suggested.

"I hope so," Frank replied somberly. "This situation has gotten out of hand."

"You're so sweet, Joe," Nancy said, sitting up in bed at the academy's medical center. "First you find that blue thread, and now flowers!"

"Go ahead and joke," Joe teased her. "You're

the one who ruined forty trainees' entire day. They canceled the obstacle course after we left. Havlicek made everyone spend four hours in the gym instead."

"And all I've done is sleep," Nancy said. "What time is it, anyway?"

"Five o'clock in the afternoon," Frank replied. "Don't worry. We've been running your errands for you. We turned in the blue thread to Agent Burr. He's having it examined, and he's already ordered a search of all trainees' and instructors' clothing."

"What about the trainees themselves?" Nancy asked. "Are they all accounted for?"

"Yes," Joe said grimly. "If one of them was missing, we'd have a lead. The agents in the field didn't find anyone with a gun, either. They didn't even find the spent shell. But rest assured, Judy is safe in her room, under armed guard."

"Well, we may not have found out much," Nancy said philosophically. "But I guess the obstacle course was worth a shot."

"You are kidding, right?" Frank replied. "You could have been killed."

"Well, I wasn't," Nancy said. She stared at Joe and Frank thoughtfully. "Actually, now that I think of it, Erin's death was the exception, not the rule. I could almost believe someone else was responsible for all the misses—the rope, the missed shots, and so on—and another person committed Erin's murder."

"Good thinking," Frank said enthusiastically. "We need to figure out what the basic difference is between Erin and the others who've been attacked."

"That may be obvious," Nancy said right away. "Jerry Nieves."

"Hey, maybe you're right," Joe said, leaning forward excitedly. "He could be the key to all of this. He knows something we don't know."

"Well, he should be at the *Observer*'s offices tomorrow," Nancy said, smiling hopefully. "Just think—with any luck, we might have this case wrapped up by then!"

"Testing, one-two-three-four." Joe readjusted the small tape recorder in the pocket of his denim jacket. "Okay, let's play that back again."

Joe pulled out the recorder and pushed Rewind. He and Frank sat side by side on Joe's bed in their room, listening to the tape.

"Do you really think Nieves is the key to either one of our cases?" Joe asked.

"Who knows?" Frank smiled as he handed the recorder back to Joe. "For now, we're working on Marianne."

"I'm glad you brought some equipment along on this trip," Joe said. "Even if I still don't understand why we're taping a conversation with Nancy's roommate."

"Nancy's convinced that Marianne is up to something," Frank reminded him. "You saw her and Banka, our prime suspect, arguing outside the gym the day Erin was shot. And Marianne has made it clear she doesn't value her colleagues much. It can't hurt to fish for clues. Think of it as a surprise for Nancy."

"Okay, fine," Joe agreed. "We might as well give it a try." He turned up his jacket collar and put his hand in the pocket, covering the voice-activated tape recorder. "We all know how popular I've become on this campus. I'll have Marianne eating out of my hand in no time."

Frank laughed. "You have your work cut out for you, Joe. She's a tough cookie."

It was just a little after seven as the boys set out for the library. Joe knew that Marianne usually studied there, even on weekends. "Break a leg," Frank said, ushering his brother inside. Joe carried a stack of textbooks he had never even opened. "I'll wait for you out here."

Inside the large, airy library, Joe spotted Marianne sitting at a study table, her furrowed brow peeking over the top of a book.

He casually made his way to the table.

Marianne raised her eyes from her book and sneered at Joe. "There are plenty of empty tables," she remarked.

"I thought you might like some company," Joe said, sitting down to face her. "That incident on the obstacle course still has everyone buzzing, but I see you're like me. Hitting the books no matter what."

"I've heard that you're not doing too well in classes," Marianne said with a cocky grin. "And now here you are, sitting beside me in the library. Not trying to spark a midterm romance, are you? You know, get the brainy girl to do your homework and then dump her after finals?"

"Come on," Joe said defensively. "I was just trying to be friendly. Sure, I could use a little help with my homework, but that's not the reason I'm sitting here. I really admire you, Marianne. Your professionalism, your determination."

"Oh, yeah?" Marianne said, setting her book aside and gazing at Joe dubiously. "Well, thanks, I guess." She stared again at her book.

Joe proceeded cautiously. "I know it's none of my business or anything, but you're not having any trouble with Banka, are you?"

"You're right, Joe. It *is* none of your business," Marianne replied.

"I saw you two arguing outside the gym the other night. It sounded as if he was trying to coerce you into doing something you didn't want to do," Joe said.

Marianne's face turned red. "Nobody coerces me into anything," she said, raising her voice. "I have to go now."

Marianne sprang up from her seat, knocking Joe's stack of books to the ground. Joe reached out and grabbed her arm.

"Marianne, wait! I didn't mean—" he began.

Marianne pushed Joe with her elbow, and to

his horror, the tape recorder slid out of his pocket. He tried to conceal it, but it was too late.

Marianne glared at him. "I don't know what you're up to, Agent Hill," she whispered harshly, her eyes narrowing. "But if you know what's good for you, you'll mind your own business!"

Chapter

Seventeen

"JOE, WHAT HAPPENED?" Frank asked as he ran into the library. "I just saw Marianne storm out. She seemed pretty upset."

Joe looked around. Several of the other NATS were staring intently at them.

"Let's get out of here," he said quietly to Frank. "And try to look cool."

As Joe gathered his things, he realized that something really was going on with Marianne. He was surprised at how angry his questions had made her, and how much angrier she'd gotten when she saw the tape recorder. No wonder Nancy was suspicious of her!

"Let's go talk to Nancy," Joe said as the boys

slipped out of the library. "I'll explain everything on the way over."

Nancy fiddled with the tuning dial on the clock radio next to her bed in the medical center. This place is so boring, she thought, stifling a yawn. There was dead silence in the corridor outside her room. Why did she have to stay overnight?

A female nurse knocked on her open door. "Agent Douglas? Agent Burr would like to see you. Can I send him in?"

"You bet!" Nancy said, brightening. She clicked the radio off. Maybe Burr had good news.

Burr stepped into the room, wearing his usual suit and carrying a briefcase. "How are you feeling, Nancy?"

"Much better," she replied. "They're just keeping me here for observation. I'm surprised to see you here on a Saturday night."

Burr smiled. "Being a special agent is not a nine-to-five job."

Nancy pointed to a straight-backed chair next to the bed. "Have a seat," she said. "I hope you're here because you have new evidence."

"Some," Burr said. He sat down and rested the briefcase on his lap. "Our forensics team made a few interesting finds this morning. I thought you might want to know about them."

"I'm dying to," Nancy said.

"First, we finally have the report on that clay you found on Marianne's glove. It appears to be an exact match with the clay found on Banka's key."

"Does that mean that Marianne is the one who broke into the gun vault?" Nancy asked hopefully.

"It could," Burr replied. "But there's one problem with that theory. She has a solid alibi for the night Erin was shot. We had fifteen NATS tell us they saw her in the gym from five to seven-thirty. Erin was shot around seven."

"She told me she was in the gym, too," Nancy said, frowning. "But what else could the clay mean?"

"I'm not sure," Burr said. "We're going to bring her in for questioning again."

"What about the cloth fibers?" Nancy asked. "Have you found the article of clothing yet?"

"We're working on it," Burr said. "Of course, chances are pretty good that it's been destroyed or thrown away. But there is one more thing—"

Burr opened his case and removed a manila folder. "Our fingerprint experts found four different sets of prints in Judy's room. We compared them to the prints we took of the NATS when they were accepted into the academy. Three of the sets matched Judy's, Erin's, and yours."

"Who did the fourth set belong to?" Nancy asked.

"Jeff Abelson," Burr said.

Nancy stared at him, stunned. "I knew Jeff was the one who ransacked Judy's room," she said with a sinking heart. Now she had no choice but to believe Jeff was up to no good.

"Now, hold on," said Agent Burr. "His prints could have gotten there for some innocent reason."

"I don't think so, sir. Jeff and Judy don't get along. If she ever invited him to her room, one or both of them are lying to me."

She remembered seeing Jeff at breakfast the day before. "It's funny," she said, "Jeff told me just the other day to watch out for Judy. He said something about her not being everything she seemed to be. What could he have meant?"

Burr rubbed his chin thoughtfully. "I'm not sure what to make of any of this, Nancy. Jeff's background is impeccable. He doesn't fit the personality profile of a murderer."

Nancy was relieved to hear Burr say so. "What are you going to do, then?" she asked.

"We'll probably question him again. Until then, we're going to continue to search for that blue article of clothing, which is probably a sweatshirt, by the way," Burr said.

"I hope we learn something soon," Nancy said. "I keep wondering when our killer will strike again."

"I understand, Nancy. I want you to know that we'll have a guard on your room all night, and Judy's, too. We don't want to take any chances," Burr said. He put the folder back inside the briefcase and snapped it shut. "Get some rest. I'll talk to you tomorrow."

"Good night," Nancy said as Burr left. As soon as I get out of here, she told herself, I'm going to question Jeff myself. I don't care what Agent Burr says. He's been behaving awfully strange lately.

She was about to turn the radio back on when the nurse appeared at her door again.

The woman was smiling. "You're our most popular patient, Agent Douglas," she said. "Agents Frank and Joe Hill would like to see you now."

"Send them in," Nancy said.

Joe plopped down on the chair Burr had been sitting in.

"What did Burr want?" Frank asked.

"He had a few interesting things to say," Nancy said. She told the brothers about Jeff's fingerprints and the matching clay samples.

Joe seemed puzzled. "I don't get that part about the clay. If Marianne didn't shoot Erin, what did she need a key to the gun vault for?"

"I'm not sure, Joe. I guess just because the samples match doesn't mean she made the key," Nancy admitted.

Frank closed his eyes. "I feel like I should know what that clay means. It's as if it's buried in my brain, and I just have to catch it, you know?" Frank said.

"Quit meditating, Frank. We've got more exciting stuff to tell Nancy about Marianne," Joe said. He explained what had happened in the library that night.

"It doesn't prove anything, but I'd be willing to bet that Marianne is involved in all of this somehow," Frank said when Joe was through. "She might even have a finger in both our cases. In fact, the deeper we get into these cases, the more convinced I am that they might be tied together somehow. If Marianne's onto us, though, we'd better make our move fast."

"That makes sense," Nancy said. "So what do we do now?"

"We tried to contact the Gray Man earlier but couldn't reach him," Frank said. "We were told we'd have to leave a message for him in Washington with a street vendor outside the Lincoln Memorial."

"I guess we'll try to go tomorrow," Joe said.

"Perfect!" Nancy said. "I'll go with you. I need to find Jerry Nieves. We'll take Judy, too. I think she's been wanting to visit her father again."

"Sounds good," Frank said. "We can take our car. Do you think they'll let you out of here early?"

"They'd better," Nancy said. "Or else I'll bust out myself!"

The sun was bright the next morning as Nancy, Judy, and the Hardys drove toward Washington, D.C. "Just stay on this highway—it leads right into the city," Judy explained to Joe, who was driving. The two were sitting in the front seat of the Hardys' compact car. Nancy and Frank sat in the backseat.

"It's a great day for sight-seeing," Joe remarked. He knew Nancy had told Judy that they were going to Washington to relax. "Can we go to the Lincoln Memorial first? That's my favorite."

"That sounds nice," Judy said. "Then, if you want, we can all meet my father."

Joe had visited Washington before, but the majestic white buildings always impressed him. From his car window, he could see the Washington Monument towering over the city.

Joe pulled up to a parking garage close to the monument, and he and the others stepped out of the car.

"We just have to walk down Constitution Avenue to get to the Lincoln Memorial," Judy said. Joe could see the white building, with its huge round pillars, straight ahead.

The day was hot, and by the time the group reached the Lincoln Memorial, Joe could see that everyone was a little worn out. Perfect! he thought. That would give him and Frank an opportunity to slip away.

"You two look like you could use a soda," Joe told Nancy and Judy. "Why don't you sit down on that bench over there? Frank and I will go find something to drink. Then we can take a look at Honest Abe."

"Great idea, Joe," Nancy said. "I could use a short rest."

Joe and Frank walked away from the girls toward a hot dog vendor parked on the grass about one hundred feet away from the memorial.

Groups of tourists, dressed in shorts and carrying cameras, were scattered around the area.

"Do you think that's our contact, Frank?" Joe asked in a low voice, pointing to the vendor.

"Let's give it a shot," Frank replied. "After your wonderful encounter with Marianne, maybe you'd better let me do the talking."

Joe and Frank stepped up to the vendor's metal cart, which was covered by a bright yellow umbrella. A redheaded woman wearing a white apron was stationed behind the cart. Joe guessed she was about thirty-five.

"What can I get you?" she asked.

"It's hot weather for a chili dog," Frank said in a low voice. Joe recognized the code they had been given the day before.

The woman's expression remained unchanged. "Will that be onions or pickles?"

"Pickles," Frank said.

"Okay," the woman replied. "Please place your order." Joe knew this was the signal to leave their message.

"We're thinking Banka when we think big cheese. Risi might be having dessert, but we think she's seen the menu," Frank said. "It's a pig-in-a-blanket, served hot."

The woman nodded. "I'll place that order," she said.

Joe had to stifle a laugh. The Network had some of the stupidest codes. Look what they had to go through just to tell them that they suspected Banka was the recruiter, and Marianne was onto their cover and was probably a recruit, and things were heating up, so the boys would need protection.

Frank started to walk away from the cart.

"Wait a second, Frank. You forgot something," Joe said. He turned to the vendor. "Could we have four sodas, please?"

The vendor was puzzled.

"I'm serious. Four sodas," he said, handing over some money. The woman took it and handed over the drinks.

"Jeez," Joe said when they were out of earshot. "I guess she thought I was still talking in code."

"Well, what are you doing, asking a Network agent for sodas?" Frank said.

"I was thirsty," Joe said. "Anyway, at least we left the message. I wonder what the Gray Man will do next."

"If I know the Gray Man, we'll find out soon," Frank said.

Looking at the Lincoln Memorial, Joe had to admit that the past could be really fascinating.

"Lincoln looks so real," Joe said as they approached the girls and handed them their sodas. "Pretty spooky, huh?" They began to climb the large stone steps toward the figure of the former president.

"The statue is nineteen feet high," Judy said. "They say that when you walk across the memorial, his eyes seem to follow you."

"Cool," Joe said. "I've got to try that!"

He ran ahead of the others to the top of the

steps. Ducking and dodging playfully, he moved back and forth in front of the statue, staring into the eyes.

"It's true!" he called back to his friends. "He's watching me. But wait!"

Throwing his weight to one side, Joe ducked around the side of the statue. He was just about to shout a joke about Lincoln not having eyes at the side of his head when he slammed into a man in a straw hat backing around the statue from the opposite direction.

"Oh, wow," Joe gasped, turning around. "Excuse me!"

He expected the other man to apologize as well. But instead, the man stiffened, pulled his hat farther down over his eyes and, in one sudden move, lunged toward Joe.

"Joe, look out!" he heard Nancy cry out. It was too late. The man's fists thudded into Joe's chest, sending him stumbling backward toward the hard marble steps. Soon Joe had lost his balance and was plunging down them!

Chapter
Eighteen

Gᴇᴛ ʜɪᴍ, Fʀᴀɴᴋ!" Nancy yelled as the man in the straw hat ran down the stairs. Joe was lying still on the eighth step down, his eyes closed, and Nancy quickly raced to his side.

"Is he okay?" Judy asked frantically as she pushed through the growing crowd around Joe.

"I don't know," Nancy said. "Joe, can you hear me?" she whispered so no one would hear.

Joe's eyes fluttered slowly open and he raised his head slightly. "I think so," he said. "What happened?"

"Somebody pushed you," Nancy said quietly. "Didn't you see him?"

Joe sat up, wincing in pain. "Oh, yeah, the guy in the hat. Where did he go?"

"I'm not sure." Nancy shaded her eyes from the sun. "Frank ran after him."

"You're going to have a nasty lump there," someone in the dispersing crowd said.

"Maybe we should find a doctor," Judy suggested.

"No, no, I'm okay, really," Joe protested. He stood up, then looked down at his jeans, which were splattered with soda. "Oh, great! That guy cost me a soda!"

Nancy couldn't help smiling at her friend. "Don't worry, Joe. We'll get you another one."

"Here comes Frank," Judy said. "He's got some people with him."

Two white-haired women wearing fluorescent pink jogging shorts were walking with Frank back toward the steps.

"Did you catch the guy?" Judy asked.

"We almost had him," said one of the women, "but we missed."

Joe gave Frank a puzzled look. Nancy could see that the older Hardy looked slightly embarrassed.

"Um, I guess I should explain," Frank said. "I was running across the lawn after the guy, and these two women thought he'd stolen my wallet. They ran after him and almost had him tackled."

The other woman nodded. "We take a self-defense class back home in Missouri," she explained.

"Loretta almost got the fella's hat off," said the woman in pink.

Her friend blushed. "Too bad I couldn't. But I'm pretty sure I scratched his face up good." She turned to Joe. "Are you sure you're all right, young man? You look a bit worse for wear."

"I'm fine. Thanks for your help," Joe said.

"We'd better be going," Loretta said. "We're going to try to see the White House today. Goodbye!"

As soon as they were out of sight, Frank turned to Joe, who was having a hard time keeping a straight face.

"Don't say it, Joe," Frank warned.

Joe was laughing out loud at this point, and Nancy couldn't help joining him. "I'm sorry. It's not every day that a pair of karate grannies come to my rescue!" Joe said.

"Maybe you could ask them for some martial arts pointers," Nancy teased.

Frank tried to act angry, but Nancy could see he thought the situation was funny, too. "You wouldn't laugh if you saw those women in action. I hope I'm still that good when I'm their age," Frank said.

Judy was the only one who didn't seem to be laughing. "What should we do now?" she asked. "Call the police?"

Nancy looked at Frank. Her instincts told her that what had just happened was no accident. Someone must have followed them from the academy. The good news was, an attack meant that the Hardys must be closer to discovering who was behind the Autowatch scam. The bad news was, it might mean their cover was blown. Nancy knew the Hardys would need to relay this latest incident to the Network.

"That's a good idea," Nancy said. "Why don't you guys go fill out a report? In the meantime Judy and I can go visit her father."

"I don't know—" Joe began, but Frank interrupted him.

"That's a great idea, Nancy," Frank said. He glanced at his watch. "It's a little after twelve now. Why don't we all meet back at the parking garage at four?"

"Are you sure you guys don't want us to wait for you?" Judy asked.

"Don't worry about us," Frank said. "You two have a good time."

"See you later, guys," Nancy said. She was sure the minute they were gone, Frank and Joe would put in another coded order with the hot dog vendor.

"I can't wait for you to meet my dad, Nancy," Judy remarked as the two young women walked away.

"I can't wait either," Nancy said. "I've heard so much about him."

"I know I talk about him too much," Judy said, embarrassed. "But you would, too, if he were your father. I'll tell you a secret, Nancy. Someday he's going to be president of the United States!"

Nancy pondered this statement while Judy

163

stopped at a pay phone to let her father know they were on their way. She wondered what Senator Noll had done to deserve such admiration from his daughter.

"He says we should come right over," Judy said when she hung up the phone. "His office is in the Russell Office Building, down by First Street. If we take a cab straight down Constitution Avenue, we can get there in fifteen minutes. You'll like the cab ride. It's almost like taking a sight-seeing tour."

"Your father is working on a Sunday?" Nancy asked as they flagged down a taxi.

"When the Senate is in session, he works practically twenty-four hours a day, seven days a week," Judy said. "Being a senator can be grueling."

Judy was right about the taxi, Nancy reflected as they zigzagged through the light Sunday traffic. She caught a glimpse of the White House on her left.

"It's hard to believe that the President could be sitting there right now, so close to us," Nancy marveled. "I feel as though I'm at the center of things in this city."

"The wildlife's not so bad, either," Judy said, giggling. She pointed to a group of tanned male tourists walking down the avenue. They were all in their early twenties. "That's the great thing about living in a place like this. There are a lot of cute guys to choose from."

"I see what you mean," Nancy agreed. She

turned to Judy. "It's good to see you smiling again."

Judy shrugged. "I guess I feel better, knowing I'll be seeing my dad soon. He and I are really close. I idolize him, really."

Nancy thought of her own father, Carson Drew, who was waiting back home for her in River Heights. "I guess my father makes me feel that way, too," Nancy said. But she wasn't convinced it was the same.

"That's the original Smithsonian building," Judy said, leaning across the seat to look out of Nancy's window.

Soon the round white dome of the Capitol came into view. The grounds surrounding the building were a brilliant green. Each tree and bush was neatly trimmed.

"These grounds were designed by Frederick Law Olmsted, the same man who designed Central Park in New York City," Judy said.

Nancy was impressed. "Judy, you really are better than a tour guide!" she exclaimed.

Judy laughed. "I guess that's what happens when you're a senator's daughter."

In a few minutes they had passed Capitol Hill and driven up to two large brick office buildings.

"Where do you want to be dropped off?" their cab driver asked.

"You can pull over here," Judy said. "We'll cross the street."

Judy paid the driver, and the girls got out of the car.

"These are beautiful buildings," Nancy said, admiring the detailed sculpture. "I suppose you know all about them, too," she added teasingly.

"A little," Judy admitted. She pointed directly in front of them. "This building was named after a former senator, Richard Russell, and the one next to it was named after another senator, Everett Dirksen. But that's really all I know."

"That's good enough for me," Nancy said. She started to step off the curb. "Let's cross. The street looks clear."

No sooner were the words out of Nancy's mouth than she heard a terrifying screech a few feet away. A black sedan peeled around the corner from behind the Russell Building and came careening down the street in their direction.

The car was picking up speed and moving like lightning toward the girls. With growing horror, Nancy realized it was headed for them. The driver was about to mow them down!

Chapter

Nineteen

Look out, Judy!" Nancy screamed. She reached out and pushed the girl toward the sidewalk. Half running, half stumbling, Nancy threw herself in the same direction. She could feel the heat from the car as it sped by, barely missing her.

When Nancy could feel the safety of the grass beneath her feet, she turned quickly, only to see the car screech around a corner and disappear.

"Are you all right, Judy?" Nancy asked. Nancy's shove had sent Judy flying, and she was sprawled on the sidewalk.

"I'm fine," Judy said as she stood up and brushed some dirt off her white shorts. "You saved my life again, Nancy. I don't know what to say."

"You don't have to say anything—at least not until we find out who's behind all this," Nancy said. "You didn't happen to catch the license plate number, did you?"

Judy shook her head. "Sorry."

Nancy stared off in the direction the car had gone. "This just doesn't make sense, Judy. Unless this is some crazy coincidence, I have to think that it must be connected with what's going on at the academy. But if Erin was the killer's real target, then why is someone still after you?"

Judy shrugged. "Beats me. I was never able to figure that one out."

"Did you tell anyone that we were coming here today?" Nancy asked.

"No," Judy replied.

"I told Agent Burr, of course," Nancy said. She thought for a minute. "Maybe we were followed!"

"That must be it!" Judy agreed. "It's the only explanation that makes sense."

"We'd better go to your father's office. We should call Burr right away," Nancy said. She brushed dirt off her own shorts, then smiled. "Remind me never to wear white while I'm on a case. I must look like a mess."

Judy laughed. "Don't worry. I'm sure my father will forgive my bodyguard for getting a little dirty while saving his daughter's life," she teased.

"Let's go," Nancy said, walking to the curb. She peered down the street cautiously. "I want to make sure there aren't any more surprises headed our way!"

Inside the Russell Office Building, Nancy was hit by a blast of cool air. Goose bumps appeared on her bare arms, but the air-conditioning was a welcome change from the humid air outside.

"It sure is quiet," Nancy said.

"It's usually pretty empty here on Sundays," Judy explained. "Most senators have houses in Virginia that they stay in when the Senate is in session, and they usually like to spend weekends at home, but not my dad."

Nancy could clearly see the admiration Judy felt for her father reflected in the young woman's face. "I can't wait to meet him," Nancy said, smiling.

Judy had the guard who was seated behind a desk inform the senator that they had arrived. The girls were allowed to get on one of the elevators.

When they stepped off the elevator, a tall, silver-haired man was standing in the hallway. Nancy knew from pictures and TV that this was Senator Noll.

"Judy! It's so good to see you," Noll said as he hugged his daughter. He released her and turned to Nancy. "This must be the world's greatest detective, Nancy Drew."

The senator was smiling, but there was something in the tone of his voice that made Nancy wonder whether the man was being friendly or if he was teasing her. "I'm Nancy Drew," she said. "But I don't think I'm the world's greatest detective—not yet, anyway."

"Don't be modest, Nancy," Judy said. She turned to her father. "Daddy, Nancy just saved my life."

The senator seemed shocked. "Are you serious, Judy? You have to tell me what happened."

What a contrast this is to Agent Burr's office, Nancy thought as she entered the senator's office. Burr's room was cold and organized; the senator's resembled a comfortable den. Thick gold carpeting covered the floor, and wooden bookshelves lined the walls.

Noll directed the girls to two brown leather chairs.

"Are you both all right? What happened out there?" Noll asked, seating himself in a chair behind his desk.

"We were crossing the street in front of the building when a car tried to run us down," Nancy explained.

"We weren't hurt, Dad," Judy quickly interjected. "Nancy pushed me out of the way. We're just a little dirty, that's all."

The senator walked over to Nancy and took one of her hands in his. "Miss Drew, I can't thank you enough," he said. "I have to say, when the FBI told me they were bringing in a teenager to look after my Judy, I had my doubts. But I was wrong. You're doing a wonderful job."

He sounded sincere—the sarcastic tone Nancy had detected in his voice earlier had disappeared. "Thanks, but I don't know if I can agree with you. I still feel as if I could have done more to help Erin Seward."

The senator withdrew his hand. "Of course, Judy's roommate. I'm so sorry," he said.

"Wait till you hear what happened at the Lincoln Memorial," Judy said. She began to relate how Joe had been pushed down the steps.

As Judy told her father the story, Nancy's gaze wandered to the senator. His bright blue eyes looked exactly like Judy's, and although his hair was gray, Nancy guessed that it had once been blond like his daughter's. It was easy to see that the two were related.

"I can't believe so much has happened to you in just a few hours," the senator said when Judy had finished.

"I have to admit it's kind of scary," Judy said, shivering a little.

Nancy agreed with her. She was beginning to think that Judy's staying on at the academy was a mistake. She thought carefully about what she was about to say. "Senator, I know Agent Burr has suggested that Judy leave the academy until the killer has been caught. After what's happened today, I think I agree with him. I'm worried that Judy isn't safe anywhere," Nancy said.

The senator stiffened. "I will decide what is best for my daughter, thank you. Judy is a Noll, and Nolls do not give in to pressure."

Even Judy seemed upset with Nancy's suggestion. "How many times do I have to tell everyone that I'm not about to leave the academy?" she said coldly.

"I'm sorry. I was just thinking about Judy's safety," Nancy said defensively.

"I understand," the senator said, softening a little. He smiled weakly. "After all, that's your job, isn't it?"

"Yes, it is," Nancy agreed. If the senator wasn't going to act in Judy's best interests, then maybe he could at least shed some light on the case. "Senator, I know the FBI has already talked to you, but would you mind if I asked you a few questions?"

The senator walked back to his chair and sat down. "It's time to play detective now, is it? All right, ask away."

Nancy was taken aback by the senator's sarcasm, but she didn't let it stop her. "I'm not sure where this fits in anymore, but do you have any idea who might want to do something like this to Judy?"

Noll leaned forward in his chair. "As you so astutely noted, the FBI has asked that question of me. And as I explained to them, every politician has enemies. But I've never been the recipient of threats of any kind, and neither has my daughter —until now."

Nancy wondered if it was worth questioning the senator further. "I understand," she said. "It's just that one piece seems to be missing to

172

this puzzle, and I thought you might know some- thing that might shed some light on it."

"I'm sorry I can't help you, young lady," the senator said. "Listen, I have some more work to do here, but I'd love to take you two out for a late lunch."

"That would be great!" Judy said.

"That sounds terrific, but I have some more investigating to do before we leave the city," Nancy said, thinking of Jerry Nieves. "Why don't you two go? I can meet you at the parking garage later."

"Are you sure you can't go?" Judy said. "It's the least we can do."

Senator Noll stood up. "Judy, I'd like to spend some time with you alone anyway. I'd like to drive you back to the academy myself," he said.

"I'll call Agent Burr and give him an update," Nancy said.

Senator Noll handed Nancy the phone on his desk. Burr sounded upset when Nancy told him what had happened, and he asked to speak to Senator Noll.

The senator listened for a minute, then began to yell into the phone, "As I've told Miss Drew, my daughter has no intention of leaving the academy!" He listened some more, then hung up. "It looks as if we'll be talking to Agent Burr tonight when I drive you back," he said to Judy.

Judy put her arm around her father. "Don't worry, Dad. If anyone can handle Agent Burr, it's you." She turned to Nancy.

"What kind of investigating do you have to do, anyway?" Judy asked.

"I need to get in touch with Jerry Nieves, that reporter from the *Observer*. I can't tell you why, but I think he might have something to do with Erin's death," Nancy said.

"Nieves? That gossipmonger? I wouldn't waste your time with that no-good excuse for a journalist if I were you, Miss Drew," Senator Noll said.

"I already told Nancy about him," Judy said. "Nancy, why are you wasting your time with that guy? Everyone in D.C. knows what a fake he is."

"I trust your judgment, Judy, but right now, he's my only hope," Nancy said. "Listen, I'd better be going. It was an honor to meet you, Senator," Nancy said.

Noll shook Nancy's hand. "It was my pleasure, as well. Don't worry, I'll deliver Judy safely to the academy tonight," he said pleasantly.

Nancy took the elevator to the lobby, then approached the security guard.

"Is there a pay phone nearby?" she asked him.

"Just outside and right around the corner," the man said, pointing.

Nancy squinted against bright sun. She felt a wall of heat as soon as she stepped out the door and made her way to the phone.

"News," a male voice answered a few seconds later.

"I'd like to speak to Jerry Nieves, please," Nancy said.

"This is Jerry. Who's this?"

"My name is Nancy Douglas, and I need to talk to you in person," Nancy said.

"Sure, you and Queen Elizabeth," Nieves replied sarcastically. "What's this about?"

"I'd rather speak to you in person," Nancy persisted.

"Sorry, but I can't help you out . . ." Nieves said, his voice trailing.

"It's about Erin Seward," Nancy said quickly.

The reporter's voice grew animated. "Are you a friend of hers? Listen, I haven't been able to get in touch with her. Is she okay?"

Nancy debated whether or not to tell Nieves the truth, then gave in. "Mr. Nieves, Erin's been killed."

There was silence on the other end of the line, then Nieves's stony voice. "Meet me at the Terminal Café in fifteen minutes," he said.

Then the line went dead.

Chapter
Twenty

THIS IS THE PLACE," the cab driver said. He pointed to the neon sign that hung above the door. The words *Terminal Café* appeared inside the bright yellow design of a computer terminal. "This is a reporters' hangout, you know. You a reporter, kid?"

"No," Nancy replied. "I'm not." Preoccupied with what Nieves had told her, she checked the meter and paid the driver.

It was about three o'clock, and the café was nearly empty. Nancy scanned the room. A gray-haired couple were seated at one table, two women in business suits were at another, but in the far corner of the room a tall, dark-haired man who appeared to be about thirty years old sat alone, nervously smoking a cigarette. He caught her glance.

Nancy approached his table. "Jerry Nieves?"

"Only if you're Nancy Douglas," he said. When she nodded, he motioned for her to sit down.

A waitress appeared at the table, and Nancy ordered an iced tea.

"You look young," Nieves said, eyeing Nancy suspiciously. "Too young to be involved in murder, anyway. What can you tell me about Erin Seward that I don't already know?"

In spite of Nieves's tough talk, Nancy detected a note of grief behind his words. She thought he was handsome, even though he was dressed in a wrinkled blue shirt, and his hair was thick and messy. Nancy wondered what Erin's feelings had been for him.

"Actually, Mr. Nieves," she began, "I came here to find out what you could tell me."

The reporter's eyes widened. "Whoa there, Douglas, first things first. For one thing, call me Jerry. For another, I want to know how Erin died. Then, if I feel like it, I'll tell you what I know," he said.

Nieves was obviously a pro when it came to bargaining for information. Nancy hoped she could convince him to talk.

"Erin was shot while jogging at the FBI Training Academy Thursday night," she said. "So far, the bureau hasn't been able to identify the gunman or determine a motive."

Nieves closed his eyes for a silent moment. Then he said sadly, "I don't know about the gunman, though I think I can help you with a motive. But what do you have to do with all of this? You're not FBI."

"Erin's aunt hired me to investigate. I'm a private detective, and I have reason to believe that you met with Erin on academy grounds shortly before her death," Nancy said. "If the FBI knew about that, they would no doubt take you in themselves for questioning."

Nancy watched carefully to gauge Nieves's reaction to her words. He didn't look intimidated, she realized. In fact, he didn't look at all like the suspicious character she'd imagined him to be. Of course, she reminded herself, looks could be deceiving.

Nieves coughed wearily. "You win, Douglas. Here's the scoop—Erin contacted me about eight months ago, just before she applied to the academy. You must know that her father lost his farm, right? Well, she said she had recently discovered something in his estate that made her believe he'd been swindled out of it," he said.

"What kind of a swindle?" Nancy asked.

"I flew out to Iowa and nosed around a bit. It was a pretty basic scam. A lawyer would be working in league with a savings and loan bank. The lawyer would convince the farmers in the area who didn't have a lot of business sense to sign mortgages that could be called in at any time."

"That means that the bank could take possession of a farm whenever they wanted to if a farmer couldn't pay off the entire loan at one time, right?" Nancy asked.

"Exactly. So after a few months, the bank would do just that. They'd get the farm and split the profits with the lawyer. It was unethical but not illegal then," Nieves said.

"That's horrible! Erin's father was a victim of that kind of scam?" Nancy asked.

"It sure looks that way. After he lost his farm, he died of a heart attack. Erin said he was a broken man."

Just then the waitress brought Nancy's iced tea. "This all happened so long ago," Nancy said thoughtfully. "Why would Erin be killed over it now?"

"Easy," Nieves said. Reaching under his chair, he pulled up a battered brown accordion folder. He opened it and took out what looked like a thick legal document. "This is a copy of the mortgage Erin's father signed."

As Nancy studied the document, she felt a surge of relief. This reporter was clearly on Erin's side, and she realized that she trusted him, too.

"There's an interesting signature here," Nieves said, pointing to it.

Nancy looked at the name scrawled in ink that Nieves was pointing to. It was easy to make out the signature: Samuel T. Noll.

"You mean *Senator* Sam Noll?" Nancy asked, shocked.

"You bet," Nieves said. "Noll was a lawyer in Iowa thirteen years ago. The dirty money he made probably financed his political career."

In a flash Nancy realized that Erin's death had nothing to do with the Hardys' Autowatch case after all. It was completely intertwined with the Judy Noll case, though—that much was perfectly clear.

A few things still don't fit, Nancy thought, her mind racing. "How do you know for sure that Noll was working with the bank?" she asked.

"This isn't the only crooked mortgage I've found with Noll's name on it. I came across at least three more, but right after I did, my files mysteriously disappeared. Erin was helping me get more dirt on the guy. She really wanted to see justice done. I'm sure Noll had something to do with her murder."

Nancy set her glass down, stunned. She found it difficult to imagine someone in Senator Noll's position ordering the death of a young woman. But then she remembered how he'd shouted over the telephone and the arrogance with which he'd treated her. She shook her head, amazed.

"I still don't get it, though," Nancy said. "If what Noll did wasn't technically illegal, why would he murder to cover it up?"

"He wants to run for president in the next election," the reporter said. "Nobody's going to elect a man who cheated hardworking farmers. His career would be ruined."

Suddenly everything became clear to Nancy. This was definitely the break she'd been hoping for. All she had to do was try to fit Noll in with the attacks, and her case would be sewn up. "What are you going to do now, Jerry?" she asked the reporter.

"I'm going to sit tight before I start talking about murder in the papers. There's not enough evidence for that yet," Nieves said. "But I think I have enough to tie Noll in to the farm scandal. That should keep the public's eyes open for a little while. I owe Erin that much at least."

Nancy was impressed. "Thanks for your help, Jerry," she said, rising from her seat.

Nieves pulled a card out of his shirt pocket and handed it to Nancy. "I'd appreciate your giving me a call if you break this case open before my people do."

"I will." Nancy tried to walk calmly out of the café, but she felt like running. It was almost time to meet Frank and Joe, and she couldn't wait to see them.

The Hardys were standing outside the garage when Nancy's cab pulled up.

"Hey, Nance," Joe said. "You saved us from another hour at the Library of Congress. Where's Judy?"

"She's driving back to the academy with her father," Nancy said. "Let's go somewhere quiet," she said. "I need to talk to you both."

"What gives, Nancy?" Joe asked once they were seated inside a small diner. "Did you find Nieves?"

"I sure did," Nancy said. "You won't believe what he told me." She explained about Noll's participation in the mortgage scam, and his connection with Erin's father.

Frank and Joe were shocked. "This means that Sam Noll had all the motivation in the world to kill Erin!" Frank said.

"It looks that way," Nancy said. She told them about their near escape on the street outside Noll's office. "Even that fits," she said. "Senator Noll was expecting us today. He could have easily hired someone to scare us to divert suspicion from himself."

A waiter came to the table with iced teas for Nancy and Frank, and a burger and shake for Joe. "I don't get it," Joe said, picking up his burger. "What about all those attacks on Judy?"

"That's the great part," Nancy said. "The attacks on Judy were like that speeding car today—they were a diversion. No one was supposed to figure out that the real target was Erin. Think about it, guys. Judy must have sneaked out of the dorm while everyone else was at the lecture that Friday evening and shot the bullets into her bedroom herself. No one was around to watch her, right? Then she ran inside and called security."

"And the gym rope?" Joe demanded. "You think she cut that halfway through herself?"

"It makes sense," Nancy said excitedly. "The only person who could be sure Júdy would choose that rope to climb—before anyone else climbed it—would be Judy herself. And as for the enlarged photograph, who could have ordered a copy more easily than the photo's owner? Judy's a top trainee, too—able to sneak around campus after hours and paste her own picture on Audrey's target, and maybe even chase her own bodyguard through an obstacle course."

"You think she did that, too?" Frank asked sharply.

"Yes, I believe she did," Nancy replied. "I was getting too close when I found those newspaper clippings in Erin's chest. That shot in the woods was Judy's attempt to scare me off. Thinking back, I honestly don't remember seeing her around just before or after we ran into the woods."

Frank stared at Nancy, aghast. "But would she do this to protect her father's reputation?" he demanded.

"Judy idolizes her father," Nancy replied. "Those are her very words. He's practically all she thinks about."

The Hardys shook their heads in amazement. After a moment Frank said, "There's still one question, Nancy. Where did Judy get the academy ammunition that was used on her room and on Erin? No one ever found an extra key."

"I'm not sure yet," Nancy admitted. "Maybe she stole bullets when she practiced at the firing range. Maybe she does have a key to the ammunition cabinet. But just because I don't know where the bullets came from doesn't mean my theory isn't true."

"You need proof, though," Joe said gently. "Otherwise, both Nolls will get away scot-free."

Nancy frowned. "I'd better call Burr now," she said, moving toward a pay phone in the rear.

Nancy called Burr's home number, and his wife answered. She said he was on his way to the academy. Nancy left a message that she would contact Burr as soon as she returned and headed back to the table.

"Let's hit the road," she said nervously. "I can't sit around eating when my case is almost solved."

Frank agreed. "While you were on the phone, Joe and I were talking over all our case's loose ends—like Banka's following us and Jeff's searching Judy's room," he said. "We figured the worst we could do is use your leftovers to figure out our own case, Nancy. To start with, we want to identify the guy in the hat who attacked us this morning. And thanks to our karate-kicking grannies, we'll be able to."

"You will?"

"Sure," Joe said. "We just need to find a guy with a fresh scratch on his face—and I'll bet my last dollar it's Mike Banka."

"Don't bet too soon," Frank said. "You're going to need that dollar to pay for that burger!"

* * *

Two hours later Frank dropped Nancy off at the administration building and parked the car in the lot near the dorm. It was six-thirty, but the sun still shone brightly in the sky.

"What makes you think Banka will be here on a Sunday night?" Joe asked as he and Frank got out of the car.

"A lot of the instructors work on the weekends," Frank answered. "It's still early. If we're lucky, we'll find him here."

"I wouldn't mind if there were a couple of Network agents along for the ride," Joe said as they crossed the campus toward the firing range. "I can't believe that hot dog vendor disappeared before we could have her tell the Gray Man we were under attack. Sometimes I hate working for top secret organizations."

The low sounds of pistols being fired echoed from the range as the brothers neared the building. "I guess some of the NATS are getting in extra practice," Frank remarked.

He entered the building with Joe close behind, and found a female special agent seated behind the counter near the ammunition cabinet.

"Is Agent Banka here tonight, ma'am?" Frank asked the agent.

"Nope. I'm overseeing practice. Is that what you're here for?" the woman asked, smiling.

"No, thanks. We just wanted to ask him a question," Joe said politely. "I guess it can wait until tomorrow."

As they left the building, Joe complained,

"Now what? We walked all the way out here for nothing. Now we have to wait until tomorrow just to look at Banka's face."

"You don't think he was hiding from us, do you?" Frank asked.

"No," Joe said, disgusted. "And even if he were, we'd have found him. He's the worst sneak I've ever seen."

"Let's go back to the dorm," Frank suggested. "Maybe the Network has tried to contact us."

As they neared the dorm, Frank noticed the back door open and an older man come out. Frank and Joe watched the man walk down the path toward them.

"Hey, Frank," Joe said. "Isn't that Professor Hoffman? Maybe we should see if he found out anything else."

Frank stopped his brother from calling out with a quick wave of his hand.

"No, Joe," Frank said, frozen to his spot. "Look—on his face."

Frank heard Joe gasp as he saw what Frank had noticed.

On the left side of Hoffman's face, clearly visible, was a long, bright red scratch.

Chapter

Twenty-One

Let's get him, Frank!" Joe said.

To Joe's frustration, Frank once again pulled him off the path and behind a tree. "Wait," Frank said in the dim light. "Let him go."

The Hardys watched the professor amble past them down the path.

"What's the matter, Frank?" Joe complained after Hoffman had gone. "He has the scratch on his face. He must be the guy who decked me!"

"If he is, that means he's onto us," Frank reminded his brother. "He wouldn't have followed us to Washington if he wasn't very interested in what we were up to. Besides," he added, "how do you know that's the scratch we're looking for?"

"I guess you're right," Joe said reluctantly. "What do you think Hoffman was doing in our dorm?"

"I don't know," Frank said, his eyes narrowing. "Let's find out."

Frank and Joe ran into the building and up to their room. The door was closed.

"It looks okay," Joe said. He flattened himself against the wall to the right of the door. "Let's not take any chances, though."

"Check," said Frank. He followed his brother's lead and stood to the left of the door, then carefully extended his hand and tried the doorknob.

"I'll turn the knob and push the door in," he whispered to Joe.

Frank reached over and gingerly pushed the door in with his foot. Then he jumped into the room, Joe right beside him. A quick glance proved that the room was empty.

"Coast is clear," Frank said.

"Let's check around. Maybe we'll find some explosives or something."

"Good idea," Frank said, and shut the door behind them. The brothers began to examine the room, which was fairly neat.

Joe was the first to catch a glimpse of white on the floor. "An envelope," he said to Frank, picking it up. "Somebody must have slipped it under the door."

"Open it," Frank said.

Joe tore open one end of the envelope, and a

small piece of paper slipped out. On it was a typewritten message. "'If you want to be where the action is, meet me on the track at ten o'clock,'" Frank read aloud. "Do you think Hoffman left this?"

Joe was puzzled. "If Hoffman is onto us, what would he want to meet us for?"

Frank shrugged. "To lure us into a trap, maybe. He might not realize that *we're* onto *him.*"

"This is too weird, Frank," Joe said. "I can't believe Hoffman is mixed up in all this. He looks so harmless. Banka is so crazy, with his angry attitude and his spying and his backfiring guns. I'm still sure he's the recruiter."

"It looks like we'll know what's going on in just a few hours," Frank said.

Joe folded his arms over his chest, and Frank recognized the determined expression on his brother's face. "Whatever he's up to," Joe said, "you can bet I'll be ready for him."

Nancy moved quickly through the administration building toward Burr's office. She hoped she had beaten Judy and her father back to campus.

The halls in the building were dimly lit and quiet. Nancy was relieved to see bright lights coming from Burr's office.

"Come in, Nancy," Burr called out when she rapped on his door.

Nancy walked into the room and was surprised to see the agent in casual clothes for the first time—neatly pressed cotton pants and a polo shirt. "Hi, Agent Burr. Did you know I was coming?" Nancy asked.

"My wife called and gave me your message. What's wrong?" Burr stood up and walked toward her.

"I found out that Erin met with a reporter named Jerry Nieves right before her death," Nancy said.

Burr's eyebrows shot up in surprise. "Jerry Nieves?" he repeated. "I've heard of him, of course. I had no idea he was working on a story with one of my trainees."

"Nieves was helping Erin get the dirt on the man who caused her father to lose his farm," Nancy informed him. "Nieves told me today that the man responsible was Senator Noll." Nancy went on to explain about the mortgage paper she had seen.

Agent Burr shook his head. "This sounds like big trouble," he said. "Bigger than I had imagined." He began pacing. "So what's your theory?" he asked.

"Erin probably suspected Senator Noll of having been the man who ruined her father's life before she came to the academy," Nancy said. "The newspaper clippings that were stored in her trunk date back quite a while. When she arrived here to begin a new life after her old dream of attending law school was crushed, she must have been shocked to find that Senator Noll's daughter was her roommate.

"Look at Erin's and Judy's files again," Nancy

urged the special agent. "It's amazing how alike they are, except for the fact that Judy had money and a father, and Erin didn't. On my first day here I was struck with how cool Erin was to Judy when Judy acted as if they were great friends."

"So?" Burr demanded. "How did Judy find out that Erin was helping research the articles against the senator? Surely Erin wouldn't have told her."

"Erin was a proud person," Nancy pointed out. "My guess is she told Judy what the senator had done, but she didn't tell her about helping with the articles. Judy figured that out by herself —first by going to the library and reading Nieves's old articles, and then by snooping around in Erin's things. After all, I saw the articles in her trunk myself."

"Yes, but then what?" Burr asked, perplexed.

"Then Judy took her news to her father, like a good daughter," Nancy said. "He said he'd take care of Erin. He came up with a plan to make Judy look like a target, and tried to make Erin's death look like a case of mistaken identity. And we fell for it—for a while.

"But Judy wanted to please her father. She decided to take matters into her own hands. She cut the rope in the gym, and put her photograph on the target. Those feats require an athletic, determined type of criminal—exactly the type Judy is."

"I follow your logic, even if there's no solid evidence yet," Burr said thoughtfully. "Nancy, I think you should know something. The reason I came to the academy tonight is because we got some word from forensics. We were able to match those blue fibers to a sweatshirt owned by one of the trainees."

Nancy couldn't believe what she was hearing. "Which one?" she asked.

"Jeff Abelson," Burr said grimly. "I never would have believed it, but we have the fingerprints in Judy's room, and now we have the sweatshirt. Not much evidence, but more than you have against Judy and her father, I'm afraid."

"What's going to happen to him?" Nancy asked, stunned.

"We plan to arrest him tomorrow morning," said Burr. "Then, of course, there will be a trial."

"He hasn't given you an excuse for being in Judy's room?" Nancy asked.

Burr grimaced. "That's the funny thing. He claims he's been watching her ever since she was shot at. Apparently Erin had said some nasty things about Judy, and he just didn't trust her. He doesn't believe Judy was telling the truth about the shooting, so he went through her room looking for evidence against her. He said he was hoping to find the ammunition cabinet key."

"Do you believe that?" Nancy asked.

"I did when he told me. Now I'm not so sure."

"But it makes sense. I remember Jeff warning me about Judy right before I was shot at on the obstacle course. And all week Judy's been telling me how crazy Jeff is about her, but it's obvious to everyone that he can't stand to be around her."

"I believe you, Nancy," Burr said impatiently, "but the solid evidence just isn't there."

"Then what do you need, a confession?"

Nancy stared at Agent Burr. Of course, she thought. Senator Noll's confession would save Jeff and neatly wrap up this case.

Burr looked Nancy in the eye. "Men less powerful than the senator have slipped through the bureau's fingers before," he said. "You've already given more than enough valuable help to the bureau, Nancy. It's time to send you safely home to River Heights."

"But I think you could use me to get Judy to confess!" Nancy said passionately. "I could talk to Judy tomorrow, before they have a chance to plan anything."

Burr sat back in his chair and sighed. "I'll tell you what. Tomorrow your group is scheduled to go to Hogan's Alley, a mock town we've constructed to enable our agents to role-play real-life situations. You can talk to Judy there. I'll see what I can set up tonight, and call you in the morning. In the meantime, we'll hold Jeff until we know what's going on. If you succeed in getting a confession out of Judy, we'll release Jeff immediately. I'm assigning a security guard to camp out in your hallway tonight," Burr said. He picked up the phone and dialed.

"Security?" he said into the receiver. "Send two agents up here, please."

"Two agents?" Nancy asked.

"One for you, and one for me," Burr said. "Senator Noll and Judy should be paying me a visit soon."

Late that night Frank and Joe stood waiting on the track near the gym. "It sure is dark out here," Joe said, peering toward the woods. "I can't see a thing."

"What do you expect?" Frank whispered. "It's almost ten. Hoffman should be here any minute. Are you sure the tape recorder's working?"

"I checked it before we left," Joe said.

In the distance Joe saw a figure approaching them.

"It could be our backup from the Network," Joe whispered.

"I don't know, Joe. That's probably Hoffman."

As the figure came closer, Joe saw that Frank was right.

"Well, if it isn't the fascinating Hill brothers. What are you two doing here this late?" Hoffman asked. He was wearing dark pants and a black sweatshirt. Even in the dark, Frank could make out the telltale scratch on his face.

"I think you know what we're doing," Joe said.

Hoffman began to circle the brothers slowly. "So, you want bigger and better things than the FBI can offer, boys?"

Frank listened in surprise. Maybe he doesn't know we're onto him, Frank thought. "We sure do," he said carefully.

"Perhaps you two would like a special assignment," the professor suggested, treading in and out of the shadows.

"What kind of assignment?" Joe asked.

"It's actually quite simple. I get you assigned to a particular watchdog team once you graduate from the academy. You sit quietly, look the other way, and accept an extra paycheck every week. How does that sound?" Hoffman said.

Frank prayed that Joe was getting all this on tape. He glanced off toward the dorm. Help seemed a long way off. "That sounds great, Agent Hoffman. When do we start?"

"Well, you could start right away," he said pleasantly. But then his pleasant expression turned into a scowl. "Unfortunately, though, we don't hire Network agents."

Uh-oh. An alarm went off in Frank's head. Our cover's blown! "What are you talking about?" he asked innocently.

Hoffman chuckled. "Nice try, Frank, but I've got eyes and ears all around this place. You two gave yourselves away days ago when you told a certain trainee that you'd missed class because you were working with me. She told me about your lie, and I got to wondering why two ambitious young men like yourselves would skip an important class and then not tell the truth about where you'd been. So I satisfied my curiosity, so to speak."

"You planted a bug in our room," Frank said.

Hoffman laughed softly. "I'm surprised it

didn't occur to you until now. After all, this is a headquarters for that sort of thing."

"You sneaky—" Joe cried, lunging for Hoffman. The older man stepped neatly out of the way, then pulled a pistol out from under his sweatshirt and waved it at the boys.

"Turn around," he commanded harshly. "Walk toward the trees. In a few minutes I'll be rid of you for good."

Furious, Frank and Joe did as they were told. Where was the Network protection they had been promised? All they could do was try to distract Hoffman.

"Why did you kill Erin Seward?" Frank asked.

"I didn't kill her. But I know who did," Hoffman said. "Those blue fibers found near Erin's body came from Jeff Abelson's sweatshirt, as our hardworking forensics technicians have no doubt discovered. In my investigation, I managed to keep a few fibers as a souvenir," he said, holding up a small plastic bag with blue threads in it.

"Soon the forensics test results will become known," Hoffman went on. "Jeff Abelson will be arrested. But before he is, he's going to perform one last double murder tonight—as these fibers will conveniently prove."

"That's pretty clever," Joe said, humoring the older man. "Too bad I didn't pay more attention in class."

Frank turned cautiously to face the professor. "Why does a brilliant guy like you need to resort to murder?" he asked, moving closer to Hoffman.

"As the saying goes, my friend, Money makes the world go round." Hoffman extended the gun in front of him with two hands. "And now I'm afraid I'll have to end this pleasant chat."

Frank was about to charge Hoffman when a small buzzing noise caught the professor off guard. "Drat, a mosquito!" the man exclaimed as he took one hand off the gun to swat his face.

Frank seized the moment. Lunging out with a martial arts kick, he knocked the gun from Hoffman's hand. Out of the corner of his eye, he saw Joe rush to tackle the professor and pin him to the ground.

"Saved by a mosquito!" Joe said breathlessly.

Suddenly the dark woods were illuminated by blinding light. Frank shielded his eyes from the glare.

"Halt!" a voice called from the direction of the campus. "You're under arrest!"

Chapter

Twenty-Two

N OBODY MOVE," the voice said again.

"It's the Network," Joe said as he stood and raised his hands in the air. Hoffman did the same.

Frank squinted, but he couldn't really make out anything through the bright light. Within seconds, a group of men and women in blue uniforms came into view.

"Not Network, Joe," Frank whispered. "Special agents."

"But what . . ." Joe's voice trailed off.

Frank saw what had startled Joe. Mike Banka was pushing his way through the group of agents, holding an open pair of handcuffs.

"Okay, Hill, the game's up," Banka said to

Frank. "Or is Hill your real name?" He jerked Frank's arms behind him and slapped the cuffs on his wrists. Out of the corner of his eye, Frank saw that Joe and Hoffman were being cuffed, too.

"Why are you arresting us?" Frank asked.

"Don't play dumb," Banka said. "The FBI's been onto this recruitment scam for months now. We suspected that Hoffman was involved, but we needed solid evidence against him. When you two clowns joined the academy, I figured Hoffman would be onto you like a fly to honey. I've been following you for days. It's a good thing I did." Banka started to walk down the path, pulling Frank with him.

"Wait! Give me a minute to explain," Frank said. "We're not who you think we are."

Banka stopped abruptly. "Oh, I think you are."

"You're wrong, sir," Joe cried from where he was standing. "We're undercover agents!"

Banka snorted. "You can tell me your fairy tale in holding."

"I think you'd better let them go," a voice said, slicing through the chaos.

Frank looked up. It was an older, gray-haired man with glasses. He looked vaguely familiar. Suddenly Frank remembered. He was the academy security guard Frank and Joe had talked to just days ago!

The man approached Banka. "Network Agent Klaver," he said. He pulled a small black folder from his pocket and showed Banka an identification card. "I suggest you uncuff these boys at once."

Banka turned pale when he saw the card. He loosened his grip on Frank, but he didn't take off the cuffs. "Mr. McFarlane? You're just a security guard," Banka said.

"Not anymore," the Network agent said. "I'm afraid my cover is useless now. But it was for a good cause. Now, can you please release these two?"

Banka's eyes narrowed. "I'll admit, your ID looks all right. But how can I be sure you're from the Network?"

Klaver sighed. "Let's go back to the administration building. A simple phone call will clear up your suspicions. Until then, I think you should stop manhandling these boys and treat them with respect. They just succeeded in cracking the Autowatch recruitment ring."

"But we—" Banka spluttered. Then his shoulders sagged. "So you beat me to it, boys," he said, turning to Frank and Joe. "Made a complete fool of me on my own turf." He shook his head. "Okay, uncuff them."

As soon as Frank and Joe were free, Joe stepped up to Banka. "You're not the only fool, sir. All this time, we thought *you* were the recruiter."

Banka stared at him in surprise. Then he laughed heartily. "No kidding! You two put on a pretty good show with your arguments about selling out."

"We were trying to attract your attention," Joe said. He motioned to Hoffman, who stood sullenly between two agents, waiting to be taken away. "When all the time, we should have been attracting *his*. But there's still one thing I don't get. If you're not the recruiter, then why were you threatening Marianne the other night?"

"I was reprimanding her. She'd been late for my class every day for a week. She claimed she had to put in extra work in forensics lab."

"Forensics? Hoffman never made us do extra work," Joe said.

Frank glanced at Hoffman, but he kept his eyes on the ground and refused to speak.

"That's it!" Frank cried suddenly. "If Marianne was hanging around with Hoffman, then maybe he was recruiting her!"

"Yeah," Joe said excitedly. "Hoffman said he had eyes and ears everywhere. Didn't Marianne catch you and Nancy talking in the lounge? She must have heard more than you thought!"

Behind him, Hoffman began coughing violently. The others ignored him.

"What are you saying?" Banka said.

"I think Agent Risi was spying for Hoffman," Frank told him. One thing he remembered made him sure: the clay Nancy had found on Marianne's glove. If Marianne had copied Banka's key, she could have jammed Frank's gun. But he didn't risk blowing Nancy's cover by telling Banka.

"Agent Klaver," Frank said, "I think I know

where we can get the evidence to sew up this whole mess. May I talk to you alone?"

"You'll talk after we make that phone call," Banka said harshly. "

Two special agents started to lead Hoffman up the path. "Good work, boys. If my hands weren't tied, I'd take my hat off to you," the older man said. Then he continued up the path.

Banka shook his head. "Now, that's sad. Hoffman had such a distinguished career with the bureau."

"Money is a powerful motive, Agent Banka," Klaver said. "I've seen this kind of thing happen to many people."

Joe turned to Klaver. "Thanks for sticking up for us and everything, but where were you when we had a gun pointed at our heads?"

"I was calling the Network for my nightly instructions at nine-thirty. The line was busy."

Joe rolled his eyes. "For a top secret agency, you guys aren't very organized, are you?"

Klaver laughed, and Frank couldn't help joining him.

"What's a security guard doing in the hall?" Marianne asked as she entered the dorm room late that night. Nancy was getting ready for bed.

Nancy shrugged. "I think they're stepping up security until they catch Erin's killer."

Marianne nodded. "That makes sense. Hey, aren't you excited about going to Hogan's Alley tomorrow? I can't wait to grab a few perpetrators. It's going to be just like when I was a cop."

"They're only regular people pretending to be criminals, Marianne," Nancy said. "Don't get carried away."

"It's all the same to me," Marianne said, flopping down on her bed.

Nancy started to get into bed, too, when she heard a loud knock on the door.

"Agent Risi! Douglas! Open up, please."

Puzzled, Nancy opened the door to find Agent Banka and Agent Burr outside. Frank and Joe were behind them with two security guards.

The group stepped into the room, and Frank shut the door behind them. Banka handed Marianne some papers. "Agent Risi, I have a warrant for your arrest for conspiring against the FBI. May I remind you that anything you say here can and will be used against you in a court of law."

Marianne turned pale. "W-what?" she stammered.

"We have reason to believe that you were involved in conspiring with the so-called Autowatch scam with Agent Arnold Hoffman," Banka said.

"Hoffman's the recruiter?" Nancy said.

"He told us about Marianne copying the key," Frank told her. "He says she keeps it in her right shoe."

Without a word, one of the security guards knelt down and removed Marianne's shoe. When he took out the key and held it up, Marianne burst into tears.

"He told me it was legal," Marianne protested. "I didn't do anything but eavesdrop a little—and once I blocked up Frank's shotgun to give him a scare. He offered me a part-time job for some pocket money. It was harmless!"

"Professor Hoffman almost killed these two young men tonight," Burr interrupted, pointing to Frank and Joe.

Banka motioned to the two guards. "Take her outside," he said.

The guards handcuffed Marianne and led her out of the room. The young woman complied silently, and Nancy couldn't help feeling a little sorry for her.

When the guards had left, Banka turned to Nancy. "I understand you helped provide a valuable clue in this case, Ms. Drew. Thank you."

Nancy looked quizzically at Agent Burr.

"I had to let Banka in on your real identity," Burr explained. "He'll be in charge of the exercises at Hogan's Alley tomorrow. I thought he should know what we're planning."

"I still can't believe Hoffman's a bad guy," Nancy said faintly. "It's all set up for tomorrow?"

"Just as we discussed earlier," Burr explained. "As you know, Hogan's Alley is a fake town set up within the real town of Hogan's Alley, Virginia. We hire local people to pose as gamblers, crooks, that kind of thing. Then NATS are sent in to 'bust' them. We've found it to be an effective method of training.

"You and Judy will be partners, and you'll be sent alone into one of the scenarios," Burr continued. "We're hoping that in such a high-pressure situation, Judy will let her guard down. If you work on it, you might be able to get a confession from her. You'll be wired, of course."

"Sounds simple to me," Nancy said.

"It's safe, too," Banka jumped in. "Besides the regular townspeople, we'll have several special agents disguised as criminals. In case Judy tries to hurt you, you'll be covered."

"I'm game," Nancy said. "Where are Judy and her father, though? Has he brought her back yet?"

"Not yet," Burr informed her. "But I'm patient. No matter how late they think they can turn up here, we'll be waiting for them."

"You're a brave man, Agent Burr," Nancy said, smiling.

"Speaking of brave," Joe said, "how about rewarding us for our bravery today?"

Banka looked puzzled.

"Let us stay on one more day and go to Hogan's Alley with you tomorrow," Joe said.

Banka looked at Burr. "They'd fit right in. As NATS, they're supposed to be there, anyway."

"All right. But as soon as it's over, I'm shipping you back to wherever it is you come from," Burr said.

Nancy smiled as Joe and Frank gave each other a high-five. She glanced at her clock. It was almost midnight. She wondered why it was taking Judy and Senator Noll so long to arrive.

"Good night, Nancy," Burr said as the men began to leave. "We'll see you in the morning."

Alone at last, Nancy changed into a nightshirt and sank wearily into her bed. When would this all be over? she wondered. She closed her eyes, and the image of Erin's lifeless body kept flashing through her mind. She was so young, and her story was so sad.

As Nancy drifted off to sleep, one thought stuck in her head—she couldn't mess up tomorrow. A girl was dead, and the Nolls would have to pay.

Chapter

Twenty-Three

Nancy shielded her eyes as the morning sun pierced the van's windows. She and nine other NATS were sitting in the back of the vehicle, dressed in tan jumpsuits and combat gear. They were heading toward Hogan's Alley, about twenty minutes from the academy. Exhausted from the night before, Nancy already felt carsick, and the day had hardly begun.

"Did you learn anything in your investigations yesterday afternoon?" Judy asked her.

"Not a thing. I didn't get a chance to do much," Nancy lied.

"Well, did you hear that Jeff was arrested? They say he's the one who was stalking me!"

"I heard that," Nancy said, "but I don't believe it." Even at the risk of alienating Judy, Nancy couldn't stand to let the senator's daughter believe that Jeff was going to pay for her crimes.

"Audrey told me about the commotion last night," Judy chattered on. "She said Marianne was arrested, too, for spying and bribery! What a class."

Nancy wanted to slug Judy. She couldn't remember when she'd felt so angry. Judy hadn't arrived back on campus until sometime after midnight, and then she'd gone straight to bed. Now she looked like a trainee with a clean conscience—throwing Nancy into uncomfortable confusion.

What if I'm wrong about all of this? Nancy wondered. The Nolls will grind me up into hamburger meat, and no one will care.

Nancy caught Judy glancing down the row of trainees at Joe, who sat holding hands with Audrey. "What's with Joe?" Judy muttered to Nancy when she realized she'd been caught looking. "Yesterday he couldn't stop talking to me. Today he doesn't know I exist."

Maybe your habit of shooting at people put Joe off, Nancy thought grumpily, but she said nothing. She caught Frank's eye, and he flashed her a smile of encouragement. Nancy felt a little better.

Nancy wished Jeff were with them this morning, flirting and joking as he always did. But

Agent Burr had arrested him, because he didn't want Judy to get suspicious.

Nancy had no more time to sulk. Through the van's side window, she glimpsed a sign that read Welcome to Hogan's Alley. Soon she felt the van pull to a stop.

The back door opened, and Nancy saw Banka there. "Okay, people, let's look alive," he said.

As Nancy climbed out, she saw three other vans pull up beside theirs. There was a different instructor with each group of jumpsuited NATS.

"Is everyone ready?" Banka asked.

Nancy casually felt for the wire that was strapped to her side. "Yes, sir," she answered, in unison with the other trainees.

"This group will be investigating a gambling operation being run out of the Dogwood Inn hotel, located at Ninety-nine Main Street," Banka said. He motioned toward three agents. "Santana, Johnson, and Klein, you'll be raiding the operation. Wallace, you'll be monitoring the radio action from the van. I want the Hills and LaFehr watching the front entrance, and Douglas and Noll out back. Got it?"

"Got it!" the group answered.

"Let's go!" Banka said.

"Are we just supposed to walk up to the hotel?" Nancy asked the other agents. "What if they spot us through a window and run?"

"Good point," Michael Santana said. "Why don't you and Noll approach the back entrance from the street behind this. We'll work out a plan for our approach from the front."

Nancy agreed, although the thought of separating from the group made her nervous.

"This place is pretty cool," Judy said.

"It is, isn't it?" Nancy agreed. The place reminded her of a movie set. There were stores and houses, and people milling about. She wished she had the opportunity to experience the exercise without worrying about having her cover blown.

I wonder how many of these people are special agents, Nancy mused.

Judy's voice interrupted her thoughts. "Nancy, I think that's the back of the hotel."

Behind a small public parking lot, Nancy could see the four-story building. A back entrance led to a yard filled with overflowing garbage cans. She guessed the door led to the hotel's kitchen.

"Should we hide behind one of these cans?" Judy asked, making a face.

"I think it's a good idea to keep hidden, but not somewhere where we can't take off after the crooks easily," Nancy said. She found a garbage can a few feet from the back door and crouched down on her heels.

"My father would scream if he knew they were giving me garbage detail," Judy joked weakly. Nancy refused to smile in return.

Besides the clanging of pots and the rush of running water, no unusual sounds were coming from the hotel. Nancy guessed it would be a few minutes before the team found the room where the gambling was going on. Now was the time to make her move.

"Judy, I lied to you back in the van," Nancy began.

"Lied? What are you talking about, Nancy?" Judy asked.

"I did make some progress on the case yesterday. I met with Jerry Nieves." Nancy glanced over at Judy, who was listening intently. "I know about your father's involvement with Erin Seward's father, Judy. I know he destroyed Erin's father, and I'm pretty sure he's responsible for her death."

Judy turned pale. "Nancy, what on earth are you saying? You're crazy!"

"I'm not crazy, Judy, and you know it. I haven't told Burr anything yet. Maybe if you go to him yourself, they won't send you to jail."

"This is ridiculous," Judy said. She was shaking. "My father couldn't have killed Erin. He has an airtight alibi for that night. You can never prove he did anything wrong. You'll see!"

If Senator Noll had an alibi, then it must have been Judy herself who had killed Erin, Nancy realized. She was glad their conversation was being picked up by the wire taped under her jumpsuit—otherwise she'd probably write this off as a nightmare.

"You killed Erin, didn't you?" Nancy said. "That's why you stayed in your room that night. You rushed back to the dorm after you shot her, and you spilled the shampoo because you were in such a hurry. Then you planted those blue fibers on the scene to frame Jeff."

As quick as lightning, Judy pulled her red handle out of its holster. She opened up the bullet chamber. "These are real bullets, Nancy. It's pretty simple to take a working gun and paint the handle red." Her voice was shaking. "I'm sorry, but it looks like I'm going to have to shoot you, too."

"Judy, are you insane? There are special agents all over this place. They'll catch you in a minute," Nancy said, trying to reason with her.

"Nothing will happen to me. My father will see to that," Judy said. Nancy realized with a start that Judy really believed her father could get her out of any situation.

Judy leveled the gun in Nancy's direction. Think fast, Nancy told herself. She caught a glimpse of a man running across the parking lot toward them. Thank goodness. It's the FBI.

But the man approaching them was pointing a gun at Nancy, too. As he reached the garbage cans behind the hotel, Nancy stared at him in disbelief. He had dark hair and a mustache, but his clear blue eyes gave him away.

"Senator Noll!" Nancy said.

"No, I'm afraid you're wrong, young lady. My name is Richard Genaro, resident of Hogan's Alley and employee of the FBI," he said. He was actually smiling. "Actually, my dear, the real Mr. Genaro won a free trip to the Bahamas recently.

He left for the airport this morning. I was conveniently able to take his place."

Nancy had to buy time. She knew that their conversation was being monitored from the van —or at least she hoped it was. Someone was sure to come to her rescue soon.

"I arranged this weeks ago as another of our theatrical events, in which Judy's life was threatened by an unknown foe. It was all part of our plan to throw suspicion off Judy. It's fortunate that we planned it," he said. "Because now I can shoot you, and Judy can claim that some madman aimed a shot at her, and you threw yourself in front of her to save her. I'll have an alibi, of course."

"I told you he'd get me out of it," Judy said smugly.

"You don't stand a chance," Nancy told them. "Nieves has the evidence to connect you to Erin Seward's father."

"I've handled more powerful people than that clown," Noll said.

Nancy thought quickly. "I'm wired," she said, lifting up the bottom of her shirt to show them. "Everything you've said is being taped."

Noll's mouth fell open but only for an instant. He recomposed himself immediately, and his voice went hard. "Thanks for telling us, Miss Drew," he said. "Now we know to take you hostage." He moved toward Nancy, carelessly waving his gun.

"Hold it right there!" a voice shouted. Nancy turned to see who it was.

"Frank!"

Noll hesitated, a confused expression on his face. Frank, Joe, and Audrey had appeared around the corner of the hotel.

In that instant Nancy took the opportunity to practice one of her self-defense maneuvers. She ran straight into the man, jamming her elbow into his gut. Noll doubled over, and before he knew it, Joe and Frank were on top of him. Frank wrestled the gun from his hands.

Suddenly a gunshot sounded, sending gravel flying out around Nancy's and the Hardys' feet. "You can't do this!" Nancy heard Judy scream. Judy was still clutching her gun.

Nancy started toward Judy, but Audrey LaFehr beat her to it. "Not so fast, Noll," she said. The agent tackled Judy around the legs, sending the young woman—and the gun— sprawling into the dirt. Nancy rushed to help pin Judy down.

As Nancy and Audrey struggled with the weeping senator's daughter, Agent Banka rushed out the back door, followed by the three NATS from inside the building.

"We heard the gunshots," Banka explained. "Is everything all right?"

"Everything's under control now," Nancy said, catching her breath. "It's all on tape—at least I hope it is!"

Banka nodded to the three trainees on the

stairs. "Santana, have the agent in the van radio Agent Burr. He's with group two. Johnson and Klein, help restrain those two. This isn't a game anymore. This is real. Let's move it."

While Johnson and Audrey handcuffed Judy, Nancy approached the Hardys. "You two saved my life. How did you know something was wrong back here?"

"Joe saw a dark-haired guy running toward the back of the hotel," Frank explained. "No one recognized him. So we decided to come back and have a look."

Banka walked up to them. "You three did a fine job today," he told them.

"Don't forget about Audrey," Joe said. "She's the one who subdued Judy."

Banka raised his eyebrows. "Really?" he exclaimed. "Agent LaFehr, you just might pass my course yet."

Instead of looking proud, Audrey's eyes welled up with tears. "I have a confession to make," she announced.

"What is it, Audrey?" Nancy asked.

Audrey burst into tears. "Those b-bullets—in Judy's gun?" she stammered. "She got them from—from me."

"What?" Frank shouted angrily.

Audrey nodded, ashamed. "We made a deal, back when the session started. She'd shoot my targets for me, from where she stood in the firing range, and I'd give her the bullets I never used."

"You *what?*" Agent Banka demanded.

"Yes, sir. I wanted to pass so much. It never occurred to me that Judy would save the bullets and use them against people."

"Of all the—" Banka looked as though he wanted to tear his hair out, Nancy noted.

"Sir," Nancy said. "She made a bad mistake. She was terrified of failing—you scared her to death."

"That's no excuse—"

"I know it's no excuse," Nancy said soothingly. "On the other hand, she's made up for it today."

Banka hesitated, glaring at the weeping trainee. Finally he growled, "You know, LaFehr, you always did baffle me."

Before Audrey could react to this sign of forgiveness, Burr appeared in the hotel's back doorway, along with some other agents.

"Take them away," Burr said, motioning to the senator and his daughter. As several agents obeyed his order, Nancy gazed at Judy's wide eyes and the senator's cold expression for the last time. "This is entrapment," the senator was saying. "You'll never prove anything!"

As he passed Nancy, the senator stopped and turned to her. "You know, I was thrilled when the bureau told me they were bringing some teenager in on this case," he said in his famous voice. "I guess I should have known better."

"You should have known better," Nancy said simply, "than to destroy innocent people's lives."

After the Nolls had been led away, Nancy's

friends gathered around her. "Why did he call you a teenager?" Audrey asked, puzzled.

Nancy looked at Burr for approval. He nodded.

"I'm not really an agent, Audrey. My real name is Nancy Drew. I'm an amateur detective. The FBI brought me on board to act as Judy's bodyguard."

"She ended up doing more than that. She solved the case for us," Burr said.

"Wow!" Audrey exclaimed. "This is unbelievable." He turned toward Frank and Joe. "And you brothers are obviously friends of hers. Does that mean you're detectives, too?"

"Yeah," Joe admitted. "But that's another story."

"Well, that explains a lot." Nancy whirled around to see Jeff Abelson, newly released, strolling out the back of the hotel. He wore jeans and a green flannel shirt, and his hands were shoved cockily into his back pockets. "Your being young, I mean," he said to Nancy. "You probably weren't ready for an attractive older man like me."

Nancy laughed, delighted to see him again. "That wasn't it at all, Jeff!" she insisted. "It's just that back home I have a—"

"Don't worry, I understand." Grinning his enormous grin, Jeff held up his hands to stop her. "I prefer women my own age anyway." He turned to Audrey. "Agent LaFehr, may I have this dance?"

Audrey laughed. "Not here, silly." She hesitated. "But if you ask me after we graduate, I just might say yes."

Burr stepped in. "You know, Nancy, you and Frank and Joe would make outstanding agents. I certainly hope you'll keep the bureau in mind when you're old enough."

Nancy was flattered. "Maybe someday," she said wistfully.

"Yeah, you know what Nancy always says," Joe quipped. *"Que será, será!"*